THE TROUBLE WITH TUCK

Other Books for Young People by Theodore Taylor

THE TROUBLE WITH TUCK

By Theodore Taylor

The author of the TEETONCEY Trilogy

DOUBLEDAY & COMPANY, INC.
Garden City, New York

Library of Congress Cataloging in Publication Data

Taylor, Theodore, 1922–
The trouble with Tuck.

Summary: A young girl trains her blind dog to
follow and trust a guide dog.
[1. Dogs—Fiction.   2. Guide dogs—Fiction]
I. Title.
PZ7.T2186Tr   [Fic]
ISBN: 0-385-17774-7 trade   AACR 2
0-385-17775-5 prebound
Library of Congress Catalog Card Number 81–43139

ACKNOWLEDGMENT

I am indebted to the Orser family, of San Francisco—
Tony, Barbara, Stanley, Leland, Scrafford, Henson, and
Gilbert—for this story. Their beloved champion-stock
Labrador, big Bonanza, became blind early in life and
mostly defied the condition. Listening to his exploits, I
was guided on tours of his haunts and habits around
upper Clay Street and in the Presidio, in the fields and
on the beaches where he romped. Though encased in
darkness, Bonanza was always a noble fighter and
dedicated lover, living to an old age, aided by a companion dog. Finally, I visited his grave on a rocky hill-
side over Pacific waters north of the Golden Gate. His
dominant personality, free spirit, pride, and dignity
served as the character model for F. T. Golden Boy.
Parts of this novel appeared in *Ladies' Home Journal*,
May 1977, under the title "Scrappy's Miracle."

THEODORE TAYLOR
Laguna Beach, California
May 1981

To my son, Michael, with love

THE TROUBLE WITH TUCK

1

No one can definitely say when Friar Tuck began to go blind, not even Dr. Douglas Tobin, who was undoubtedly one of the best veterinarians in California. But the light probably began to fail for big Tuck long before any of us suspected it, and of course, being a dog, he couldn't very well talk about it.

I suppose that exactly when the shadows began creeping in, or when he finally slid into total darkness, doesn't really matter.

Yet I can clearly recall that miserably hot summer day so long ago when we first thought something might be wrong with Tuck. It didn't seem possible. Young, beautiful, so free-spirited, he had a long life ahead.

But the August of Tuck's third year on earth, my father, an electronics engineer, flew to Chicago on business, and the next day, a Monday, about midmorning, some neighborhood cats got into a noisy brawl along our back fence, spitting and screeching.

To Friar Tuck, that was always an unpardonable sin. Not only were these cats intruding in *his* yard, a private and sacred kingdom, but, worse, they were creating an ear-splitting disturbance. His answer was immediate attack, as usual.

My mother was in the kitchen at the time and heard him scramble on the slick linoleum, trying to get traction with his paws, and as she turned, she saw him plunge bodily through the screen door, ripping a gaping hole in the wire mesh.

Up in my room, making my bed as I remember, I heard her yell, something she seldom did, and, thinking she'd hurt herself, I hurried downstairs and out to the kitchen.

Mother was standing by the back door, looking outside, puzzlement all over her face, which was usually a mirror of calmness. She still had her hand on top of her head, having forgotten it was there. Putting fingers to her hair was a familiar gesture when calamity occurred.

"Tuck just went through this door," she exclaimed, unable to believe it. The hand came down slowly. "I declare." She was a Southern lady but had lost most of her way of speaking.

I then saw the big hole in the wire, as if something had exploded there.

"Some cats were fighting, and he got up and ran right through the door." Mother was awed.

I was sure that Tuck was far too intelligent to do a stupid thing like that. He'd always put on skidding brakes and just barked loudly if there was something outside disturbing him.

I said, "Maybe he was dreaming?"

Mother scoffed, "Helen!"

All right, he wasn't dreaming. He'd done a very dumb thing.

I looked out at him, thinking about excuses.

Tuck was sitting innocently on his powerful haunches in the grass, that dignified lionlike head pointed skyward. He seemed to be sniffing the air as if to make certain the squabbling cats had departed. To be sure, he wasn't concerned about any whopping hole in the screen door.

My mother shook her head and went outside, quickly going down the short flight of back steps and crossing over to him, maybe to scold him properly. He deserved it.

I followed her.

As she approached Tuck, his thick tail began to wag, switching back and forth across the grass like a scythe. She said, "You silly dog, you just broke the door," leaning over to take his big yellow-haired head into her slender hands and examine his eyes. She bit her lip and frowned.

Wondering why she'd done that, I had the strangest feeling.

Mother straightened up, still frowning widely.

"Why did you do that?" I asked. "Look at him that way?"

"Well, he acted as though he didn't even see the door."

Now it was my time. "Mother," I scoffed.

Then I went over and peered down into his eyes. To me, they were the same as they had been for more than three years—liquid deep brown with dark pools in the center. They were so expressive, in laughter or sadness.

"Have you noticed anything different about Tuck lately?" Mother asked.

"What do you mean?" He hadn't been sick or anything, to my knowledge.

"Oh, just anything different."

Offhand, I said, "No."

But there was something, now that I thought about it. I glanced into the acacia trees at the back of our deep lot. Doves often roosted up there, cooing in the day hours, and then they'd drop down to the yard and peck around. Tuck had always chased them, in rousing good fun and fair game, never catching one. They'd fly up and scatter, terrified of the bounding dog with the deep-throated bark. He loved to do it.

However, a while back, maybe three months earlier, the doves had suddenly turned defiant, I'd noticed. They'd begun to parade brazenly across the backyard. And I'd also noticed that Tuck wasn't going after them anymore. Maybe he was just bored with them, I thought. Or maybe the doves knew something that we didn't. I didn't want to think about that.

I said, "He's quit chasing the doves."

My mother's laugh was hollow. "I don't know what that means."

"Neither do I," I said. Maybe he was just lazy in the heat.

She sighed and went back to the door and stood

there for a moment, staring at it, then shook her head
and went on inside.

Thinking about the crazy thing that had happened
in the morning, I took Tuck for his regular afternoon
walk that humid day, paying special attention to what
he did. That turned out to be absolutely useless because he did the same old dog things he always did—
sniffing his way by the telephone poles and fire hydrants when we were going along the sidewalk; more
sniffing and running and endless leg lifting in the
park, branding his territory.

However, it did seem to me that he was walking
with much more care than I ever remembered. In the
past, he'd moved along as though he owned the sidewalk and street and all the greenery in the park.
Those muscular legs pounded down from his wide
chest and hindquarters with great authority. He
walked the way a giant walked, very chesty.

Yet Luke, my youngest brother, sometimes accused
me of inventing weird things in my head. So maybe I
was just inventing this trouble with Tuck? Maybe he
really had been dreaming—dogs do dream—and was
chasing cats in this dream, and woke up, and without
thinking rammed right through the door. There are
good excuses for almost everything, I've found.

When I returned home in the late afternoon,
Mother asked, "You solve the mystery of the door-
breaker? I should make him pay for it." She was reading on the chaise lounge in the backyard shade, trying
to keep cool. She rested the book, studying Tuck, who
was slurping water.

I said I hadn't solved the mystery. "The only thing

he did different was to walk right by the Leonards' old Maltese. It was under their car."

"He didn't see it?"

"I guess not."

My mother made one of her distinctive "hmh" sounds, which always indicated she'd think about the subject for a while. Then she picked up her book again.

A little later she came into the house and summoned me to the kitchen. "I want to try something," she said. "Bring Tuck in here."

He was by the garage door, sprawled out asleep on the concrete, which was in cooling shadows. I whistled for him, and he rose up, stretched lazily and luxuriously, then meandered into the house, probably thinking it was mealtime.

There was a round oak breakfast set in one corner of the large kitchen, and Mother placed one of the ladderback chairs about three feet away from the screen door.

Holding Tuck by the collar, she instructed, "Helen, go outside now."

I did so.

"Okay, make him come to you."

That was usually easy. All I had to say was, "Tuck, let's go." He was always ready to go. Anywhere.

This time, when I called, though, my handsome thoroughbred dog headed for the back door and ran headlong into the tall chair, spilling it with a clatter.

It was obvious he did not see it.

I heard Mother's dismayed voice from the kitchen. "Oh, no."

By that time, I was opening the door, and Tuck was standing by the knocked-over chair, staring in my direction, quite confused.

I said to my mother, "Something must be wrong with his eyes." I now had to admit it. My stomach was suddenly cold and empty.

She nodded. "I think so too. I'll make an appointment with Dr. Tobin for Saturday morning. Your father comes home Friday night."

All week I worried and kept looking into Tuck's pupils for answers that were not there.

2

As a child, I lived at 911 West Cheltenham Drive, in the aging Montclair Park section of Los Angeles, in a large, very comfortable two-story white clapboard house, built around 1920 when there were orange groves not far away and blue skies were really sky-blue.

Upstairs there were four spacious bedrooms, including mine; two baths, each with claw-footed tubs; and a wonderful attic, in which I spent much time looking at old scrapbooks from my father's South Dakota family. A man from Minnesota had built the house, and there was even a basement, a rarity in Southern California.

Downstairs was the living room, with a wide brick fireplace; the den, with another fireplace and many bookshelves; the dining room; and the roomy kitchen, which looked out on the backyard. The kitchen had a built-in ironing board and a "cooler" cupboard where the owners kept potatoes and other vegetables back in the 1920s. It was a fine house in which to grow up and have a dog.

There were manicured lawns front and back, and Mother grew many flowers in the beds that bordered them. A white board fence about four feet high encircled the backyard, and a driveway lay along the entire west side of the house, ending in a two-car garage.

It was up that driveway that my father's new red MG came, honking twice, on a bright October afternoon in the early 1950s, when I was nine and a half years old. High winds and early fall rain had chased the smog out of the Los Angeles basin, I remember, leaving the city unusually bright and clear. To the east, the Hollywood Hills and Santa Monica Mountains were sharp against the horizon.

About four-thirty, my father eased to a halt within a few feet of the garage and climbed out, elaborately carrying something light gold in color. Seven weeks old, just weaned from proud Maid Marian, who'd won more than a dozen national show ribbons, the pup was a squirming fat sausage of creamy yellow Labrador.

Anticipating my joy, my father was elfish and smiling, holding the furry ball as if it were an offering.

I ran across the yard and scooped the tiny thing from my father's hands as he announced, "All yours, Helen. Not for Stan or Luke, or me, or your mother." Stan was my oldest brother, an ancient thirteen. Luke was then a troublesome eleven.

I was almost speechless.

The pup was making tiny yelping noises, as if anxious to place his feet safely on the ground after the ride from the kennel. He was mostly belly.

I was stunned.

Watching me closely, enjoying my surprise, my mother stroked the pup's head and talked about big responsibilities. "Now, you'll have to feed him and bathe him and take him to the vet's."

That was so typical of her. She was always one to keep things in order. She was auburn-haired, very pretty, and had a good figure for her age, which was late thirties. She taught school, the elementary grades, in the winter months. My father, bespectacled, balding, and pudgy, was not nearly so orderly at home, even though he was an engineer. And he liked to surprise us all now and then. That day was a "now" for me.

I guess the advice they freely gave was standard for the occasion: He's all yours, and *you* better take care of him. That was fine with me.

I hugged the soft yellow warmth that October afternoon, so surprised that I'd been presented a dog. It wasn't my birthday, or Christmas, of course. My cat, Gray Rachel, had been run over the previous year, and I still grieved for her, but that wasn't the reason Friar Tuck came into my life. I didn't learn the reason until much later. At that moment, I was just content to cuddle the pup and give reverent thanks to my parents, whatever their reason or the occasion.

Up on the wall of what was my childhood room at 911 West Cheltenham is a large photograph of myself and two big dogs in the thick green grass of our backyard. I'm smiling and kneeling between Tuck and another dog, Lady Daisy, a serene German shepherd. She is also a part of this story, perhaps the most important part.

We're looking straight into the camera, and that blown-up, grainy photo, easily two feet by two feet, taken by my mother so long ago, holds many memories, some as sharp as yesterday.

Anyone examining that picture can see I was not very pretty, to say the least. My mouth was too large for my jaw. My nose was puggy and freckled. My grin exposed crooked teeth with wire braces on them. I was wearing glasses, as I do now. Oh, how I hated those glasses and the mean braces. Not helping the above appearance, I was painfully skinny, with knobby knees and sharp elbows. Back then, girls did not wear jeans very often, and there was no way to hide my spindly legs. I was often ashamed of them.

Roundly cheated by nature, I was understandably shy and sometimes stayed in a shell of my own making. When I came out, I did something that almost drove everyone crazy. I whistled. Oh, how I whistled. I whistled indoors and out until one or another member of the Ogden family would shout, "Will you stop it, Helen?"

Most of the time, I didn't even realize I was whistling. I'd stop, but then I'd start again, unawares.

The constant tweeting was a habit, like chewing fingernails, and a psychologist had told my parents something I wasn't supposed to know: I had no self-confidence, and that's why I whistled.

Did he really think I didn't know I lacked confidence?

What made it all worse was the fact that both Stan and Luke were handsome and fine athletes, while I was cloddish-looking and about as coordinated as a day-old ostrich.

Truly, there were moments when I gazed into the mirror at my wide mouth and brick-red hair, not that fine auburn stuff my mother had on her head, and wondered where I had come from. There were moments when I wanted to die, like the moment I was carrying Luke's eleventh birthday cake into the dining room, singing the birthday anthem, and stumbled. I went face-first into the icing and candles.

Only in the movies is that supposed to happen.

3

As if describing royalty, my father said, "The pup has papers, Helen. That means his bloodlines are recorded by the kennel association. You can breed him someday, if you'd like. Maybe have champion stock, the same as his mother."

As little as he was, he looked like champion stock, all right.

But my father added slyly, "There's also a possibility that he may be flawed."

"What do you mean?"

"See that pinkish tinge on his nose, just at the end. It could go away. Maybe not. If he has pink on his nose when he's older—it's called a Dudley nose—you'll never be able to show him. His nose has to be pure black to compete."

I laughed.

Who cared about a pure black nose? Who cared

about a Dudley nose? I wasn't concerned about breeding him or showing him. Just having him was enough.

Of course, there was no way to see the other terrible flaw that lurked within him.

Predictably, my mother asked, "What will you name him?"

Having owned him less than ten minutes, I hadn't thought anything about names. But it was very important that he have the exact right name. A "Rover" or a human name like "Jack" would never do.

Pulling the kennel papers from his coat pocket, displaying them, my father said, "His sire is named Gold Mack, and his mother is Maid Marian Golden Girl. I've met her, and I saw a picture of Gold Mack. He's a beaut. Very big and husky. Between the two of them, you should have a great dog."

There was little doubt about that. "I'll have to think of a good name for him," I said.

My mother asked, "Have you ever read *Robin Hood*? It's in the den."

I knew about Robin Hood, of course, and I had leafed through the book looking at the pictures. But already I didn't want my dog to have a robber's name, good robber or bad robber. He should have a noble name of some kind, I believed. Maid Marian certainly had an aristocratic family ring to it.

"How about Little John?" my mother suggested.

Father laughed. "He'll be anything but little."

Having accomplished their mission, the bestowing of an animal upon me for reasons unknown, my mother and father went on into the house, but I stayed outside for almost an hour, playing with the pup in the damp grass. His legs were so short that his near-bursting belly dragged across the blades. I tumbled him about, letting him chew on my fingers and shoes.

Once, I held him up at arm's length and examined him in detail. I could swear, even now, that he had a very real smile on his tiny face.

And if there was anything better to hold than a pup, I didn't know what it was. I put him up to my shoulder, against my neck, and his warm tongue swabbed the lobe of my ear. His new fur was like velvet.

A love affair began that hour.

I went to the garage and found an old towel that Stan used when he washed my mother's station wagon. I dragged the growling pup around the yard, his pin teeth locked on the cloth. If he missed his mother and littermates, he didn't show it that early evening.

Luke came home first, after playing soccer.

"Whose pup?" He was always abrupt.

Luke had a good-boned face, like my mother, and straight, shining teeth, and didn't need to wear glasses.

"Mine," I answered in kind.

"Who gave him to you?"

"Mom and Dad."

"Why?" Luke should have been a lawyer.

How should I know why? I often got exasperated with Luke, and he with me.

"Because they wanted to."

"Hey, he's cute."

It didn't take a qualified genius to see that.

Luke dropped down on his hands and knees, tussled the pup for a few minutes, and then went on into the house to take a shower.

Then Stan came pumping up on his bike. He bagged groceries after school at the supermart over on Beverly.

"When did you get the pup?" Being older than Luke, he was nicer than Luke.

"This afternoon."

"Where'd it come from?"

"Mom and Dad."

"It's not your birthday, is it?"

"No." I wouldn't be ten for another five months.

Stan shrugged and then knelt down to play with "Nameless," yelling and laughing when one of the sharp teeth clamped on his finger. Almost six feet tall, Stan always intimidated me, just by patting me on the head. He, too, had straight, shining teeth, and he got love notes from girls in junior high. I knew. I'd read them. Stan went on into the house.

I stayed outside until darkness began to lower over the Santa Monica Mountains and the air became chill. Then I lifted the newest member of the Ogden family and proceeded into the kitchen, somehow feeling different than when I'd awakened in the morning. I now owned something that was living and breathing.

My father had brought home formula food from the kennel, and after licking the bowl clean, the little dog, exhausted from the afternoon's events, found a place on the linoleum near the oven's side exhaust and went to sleep. On request from my mother, I awakened him immediately to take him outside for a squatting session. Then I put him down again by the oven.

At dinner, the name game began once more.

Stan, with his mouth full of squash, suggested I call him Friar Tuck, from *Robin Hood*.

I looked over at Maid Marian's infant son, who'd just awakened. He didn't resemble Friar Tuck, who was old and fat.

I said, "No."

"How about Mack, Junior? After his father?" my own father suggested.

I don't like "junior" names, human or canine.

Stan said, "Hah, hah, how about Mack Truck?"

Luke, whose mouth was also full of food, as usual, said, "Call him Poopy. That's what he's doing now."

I looked over and jumped up from the table.

By bedtime, the new canine member of the Ogden clan was officially christened Friar Tuck Golden Boy, after my mother pointed out that I didn't need to call him Friar unless I wanted to. Tuck, we all agreed, was a suitable and noble name, without getting fancy.

After being awakened for his formal christening, he was soon asleep once more, this time in my old playpen, dragged out from the garage and carpeted with newspapers. The playpen was placed in my room, near my bed, and my father put a windup clock and a hot-water bottle in it for the prescribed ticking sound and warmth, although Tuck still hadn't yowled for Maid Marian.

My mother, who was not one of those fussy nervous

housekeepers but did jealously guard her rugs and furniture, made it plain that housebreaking would start the next day. But she had no objections about Tuck staying in my room.

Just before I switched off the light, I said to my new roommate, who was showing a great talent for sleeping, "I'm so glad you're here."

Looking back, I see it was the start of a "new" me.

4

By the time Friar Tuck Golden Boy was three months old, he was completely housebroken, and the playpen had been put back into storage, awaiting chance visitors with babies or, way down the line, grandchildren.

Because he'd become "civilized," Tuck was now a permanent night resident in my room, and although I maintained to everyone that he slept strictly on my bedside rug, there wasn't a single night that I couldn't feel his weight at the end of my bed, often a cozy lump over my feet. He was my security in the darkness, my knight of the night.

One black, scary hour, during a rare thunderstorm over Los Angeles, with lightning cracking and great rumbles of thunder shaking the house, I let him sneak under the covers with me. No, I won't lie. He was invited under many times, especially when I'd had a bad day. I know that many other people do this, and just ignore the fleas, as I did.

Tuck had his bad days too. He made ribbons of an expensive Norwegian wool sweater that my mother had put out to dry in the shade. He also ripped out some of her best plants. But these are normal puppy happenings, and anyone with a right mind would understand them.

By now, the Dudley pink was confirmed and had enlarged to cover about half of his nose, making it mottled black and pink. Though it wasn't a shocking pink, it was pinkish enough, and Tuck could never be entered in one of those ritzy dog shows and win ribbons. That bothered me not at all.

Something else had been confirmed. That tiny smile I thought I'd seen on his face as a pup, like the smile of a baby with gas pains, was also enlarged and really there. A friendly human face approaching Tuck was rewarded with a genuine smile and sometimes a dancing of front paws.

Soon we were a team, the dog with the Dudley nose and wide smile and dancing feet, and unglamorous me. I couldn't wait to come home from school each day, knowing that we'd go off somewhere together—often to the park, or to a friend's house, or just for a long walk around the blocks that bordered our own. During the school hours, when no one was at home, he stayed peacefully in our yard with the pestering doves, hemmed in by the fence. He hadn't learned to jump it yet.

Already he'd begun to develop certain habits—sleeping in special places indoors and out; awakening

me each morning in a special way, putting a paw
against me and shoving. If I didn't respond, he'd go
into the next room and arouse my mother. He had lo-
cated the cookie jar in the kitchen and sat before it
expectantly as soon as I came home from school. We'd
each eat a cookie, and then off we'd go into the wide,
wide world of fire hydrants and bushes.

On coming back from the park, we'd usually stop
by Ledbetter's, the independent grocery store in the
small Rosemont Street shopping center near us. We'd
visit Mr. Isoroku Ishihara, who had charge of the veg-
etable counters that were rolled out to the sidewalks
each day. Ledbetter's was known for its fresh fruits
and vegetables, arranged like green and red and purple works of art in the bins. Mr. Ishihara, a small man
with crisp gray shining hair and skin the color of
polished walnuts, always had something nice to say
about Friar Tuck.

"My, how he's growing."

"He's thirty pounds now."

"You must use a good shampoo on his coat, Helen.
It gleams."

"I use my own." My relationship with Tuck was always very personal.

Mr. Ishihara would laugh and dig under his lettuce
bin for a dog biscuit. He fed all the neighborhood
hounds. His own pet was an old alley cat named
Ichiban, which means Number One in Japanese.

After visiting Ledbetter's, Tuck and I would continue on home, whistling the tune of the day. There
was one L.A. station, KFWB, that always played the
hits, and I'd listen almost every afternoon, sprawled

out on my bedroom floor. Rock and roll was just coming in, as was Elvis Presley.

At home, I often talked to Tuck, telling him things
I'd never tell anyone else. Sometimes I read to him,
but he usually frustrated me by going to sleep.

I remember taking *The Adventures of Robin Hood*
down from one of the long shelves in the den and
reading to him Friar Tuck's first speech of the book,
when King Richard came to Sherwood Forest:

"'Take care whom thou pushest against!' cried a
great, burly friar. 'Wouldst thou dig thine elbows into
me, sirrah? By'r Lady of the Fountain, if thou dost
not treat me with more deference, I will crack thy
knave's pate for thee . . .'" I paused.

"That was you," I said to my roommate, but he'd
gone off to sleep, curled up like a bear cub.

When Tuck was six months old and weighed up-
ward of fifty pounds, whatever my mother and father
had plotted must have been working because one
night my father said, "You've certainly done wonders
since you got that dog."

I was very pleased.

Of course, I thought he was talking about all the
training I'd been doing, how Tuck had learned to heel
and stay and play catch. But that wasn't what my father was talking about at all, I soon learned.

One afternoon, when we were alone, having lunch
out after we'd gone shopping, my mother said,
"Helen, you seem confident for the first time in your
life. I can see it even in the way you walk."

"How did it happen to me?" I asked, really wondering how.

She laughed. "Well, we think it's Tuck. We have no other explanation."

I hadn't thought about it. Yet it was all happening naturally. Yes, some chemical had mixed, thanks to Tuck, and I was blossoming at last, I guess. I could almost feel it. I was ten by now. The psychologist could go pound sand.

Even Stan and Luke had something to say about it, though grudgingly. "She doesn't whistle half as much since she got that dog," Stan said at the breakfast table.

My mother sighed. "Can't you say something besides 'she'? Helen *is* here at the table—in the flesh!"

"Oh, Mom, *her*." He pointed.

Luke said, "Tuck takes her mind off her mouth."

I wanted to smack both of them but never had the courage to try.

When Tuck was nine months old, just before school let out for the summer, I could see how he would look for the rest of his life. By then, he was powerfully built, with a wide chest and well-sprung ribs and loins that were heavy and solid. His hindquarters were muscular, and his legs straight from shoulder to ground, with heavy bones. His paws were compact and thickly padded, toes perfectly arched and hocks well-bent. His dense short coat appeared to have been dipped in twenty-four-karat yellow-gold.

However, as much beauty as there was in his supple body, it was Tuck's head that caused people on the street to stop us and marvel. I felt so proud of him. He carried that massive head, even as a young dog, with the air of a lion. And his tail never drooped. It was always up, like a yellow flag.

There's another picture up on my childhood wall. My father shot that one at the beach when Tuck was ten months old. I'd thrown a ball, and Tuck was photographed leaping straight up in the air, catching it, all four feet off the ground, like one of those circus dogs, though I never taught Tuck to do tricks. That was below his dignity.

He did his own tricks, anyway. About that time, Tuck began to steal things from me and hide them. A shoe. A sock. A belt.

At the clinic for Tuck's rabies shot, I asked Dr. Tobin why he was doing it. The doctor laughed and said, "Because he loves you. He only has so many ways to show you. Taking your things to keep near him is one of the ways."

Stealing? I forgave him.

In September, when Tuck was one year old, he showed his devotion in another way, and I became indebted to him for life.

We went along to the park one late foggy morning, and as usual I let him off the leash just as we reached the wide entrance. Montclair Park, which covers almost five hundred acres, with a small lake in the center, has many shade trees, and I'm sure Tuck managed to lift his leg to most of them at one time or another.

I was always content simply to walk along behind him wherever he went. Usually he'd look back every now and then to see that I was still there. I never had any worry about him running away, though he was becoming more and more independent when I wasn't around. He could easily leap our backyard fence now.

But on this particular morning, the fog was very heavy, and I soon lost sight of Tuck, who was busily going from bush to tree. One thing I knew was that he could always find me.

Suddenly, out of nowhere, appeared a slim man in a light blue jacket, khaki pants, and a baseball cap. He smiled at me and said, "Hi, little girl."

My heart began to thump.

I didn't see anyone else around. In good weather, there were always older people sitting on the benches or sprawled out on the grass, reading or talking. Kids went through the park on bikes. Mothers pushed baby strollers along the walks. Often, there were workmen around, trimming the bushes or cutting the grass or emptying trash.

Today, not a soul.

I didn't like the way this man was looking at me, either, with a funny wet grin on his narrow face. His eyes were bright—too bright. I'll never forget his thin face. It was like a wedge.

He asked, "Where ya goin'?"

Not answering him, I started to walk very fast, and he followed, into the dense fog.

Starting to run, I heard him running behind me, through the swirling mist. I desperately yelled for Tuck. No sooner did I do that than the man caught up with me, grabbed me, and put a hand over my mouth.

I remember that I tried to pull his hand away by

jerking at his wrist, but he had me tight around the neck in the crook of his arm, as well as around the waist. I was helpless, and he seemed to drop to one knee. He ripped at my dress.

At that moment, there was a roar and an explosion of gold that jarred me loose from his arms.

Tuck had hit the man from behind, leaping on his back, jaws wide.

There was a wild tangle, and the man screamed, trying to push the big dog away. With Tuck snarling and biting and the man screaming, the sound was terrible, and I crawled off, feeling sick.

All of it stopping as suddenly as it had begun, Tuck soon came over to me, flecks of blood around his nose and in the yellow hair on his chest. I saw the man get up and run off into the mist, bent over, holding his shoulder and neck. He wasn't moaning or anything. His baseball cap was still on the ground.

Then I stood up, shaking all over, my heart still thudding, and hooked the leash into the ring on Tuck's collar, and we hurried out of the park. I was not whistling.

I knew what had almost happened to me, knew what that man had intended to do, and Tuck was a hero around our house that night and forever after.

Thankfully, I never saw the man in the blue jacket and khaki pants in Montclair Park again.

5

If there was ever any doubt whatsoever about the special status of Friar Tuck Golden Boy at 911 West Cheltenham, no matter what he did or didn't do, the doubt was removed the following summer when Tuck was nearly two years old.

On a July morning, with the temperature climbing toward a hundred, I went to Steffie Pyle's house about a half mile away, to swim and just goof around. Though I'd joined Stan and Luke and my mother in campaigning for a pool, regretfully there was none in our backyard, so Steffie invited me over regularly during the summer and early fall.

Both the same age and suffering from equal injustices of nature, we'd been good friends for a long time. Steffie was also cursed with silver braces on her teeth and glasses on her nose. She had even more freckles than I did, and where I was skinny she tended toward fat. We sometimes compared notes and wondered how we could have such pretty mothers and still look as though we came from the zoo. Maybe our fathers had done it to us.

Steff's father had been on the diving team in college, and the board at their pool had a lot of spring. It was fun to jump up and down on it, get tossed high into the air, then do a bottom-buster into the water.

I was doing just that, springing maybe three or four feet into the air, trying to go even higher, when I lost my balance, missing the end of the board with my feet but hitting the back of my head on it. Everything went black.

What happened right after that was told, and retold, first by Mrs. Pyle, then by Steff, then by a lot of other people, and finally by the costar of it all—me.

When she saw me go underwater and not come up, Steff seemed to be paralyzed except for her vocal chords, which was fortunate. She could see me down on the blue pool bottom, looking asleep or dead, but somehow poor Steff couldn't move. She was a frozen ninny there by the pool, just screaming.

According to Mrs. Pyle, who was in an upstairs bedroom when it all happened, she heard this high, long insane scream, an "ahhhhhhhhhhhhhhhhhhhh," as if Steff had caught her thumb in a car door. When Mrs. Pyle heard it, knowing we were at the pool, she ran down the steps, through the dining room and kitchen, and out the door.

But by that time a smart dog named F. T. Golden Boy had already dived into the water, swum down to the bottom, put his jaws around my upper left arm, and paddled to the surface.

Mrs. Pyle jumped into the water with all her clothes on and relieved Tuck of his unconscious burden—me.

Slapping Steffie to jar her back to her senses, Mrs. Pyle sent her to the phone to call the fire department, while she gave me artificial respiration at poolside.

The rescue squad and paramedics arrived a little later, but by that time I was breathing all right and coughing and puking all over the white tile. Meanwhile, Steff helped Tuck, the lifeguard, out of the pool. He'd been paddling around for almost ten minutes and must have been pretty tired.

I spent the rest of the day and night in the hospital, while the doctors checked for concussion, which I had slightly, and any other damages. They were mostly to my ego. Of all the people involved, I was the least informed. After banging my head, I don't remember anything except waking up and puking.

To the whole world, at least my world, I had proved once again that if there was a way to mess things up, I'd find it. Although there was concern and sympathy for me at the hospital, even from Stan and Luke when they visited, my yellow dog was the star of the entire affair, rightfully so.

In fact, Tuck was now something of a recognized hero in the park and along the streets of the neighborhood. Professionally trained dogs did stunts like that, we were told, retrieving objects in dives of eight or ten feet, but Tuck was one who hadn't been trained and had made a rescue purely by instinct.

Maybe it was silly to keep thanking him, but I did, with words and hugs. He surely understood the latter.

Although the escape from drowning made me considerably more careful around diving boards and pools, or in the ocean at Malibu, where we sometimes went on weekends, Tuck's own life remained much the same, as expected. He came and went as he pleased, staying mostly in our backyard but going off on personal adventures now and then. He continued to cheerfully chase the cats and doves if they trespassed on his property, remaining the barking guardian of all he surveyed.

Summer, winter, spring, or fall, Tuck would take an early morning stroll by himself, trotting about the neighborhood, or he might go to the park, skillfully avoiding the traffic. Sometimes he'd visit Mr. Ishihara at Ledbetter's. All things together, he'd turned out to be one of the most independent dogs that ever lived.

Yet he was so alert and intelligent that none of us ever really worried, even when he crossed streets that were heavily traveled. He was seldom away more than two hours.

On many occasions, Tuck seemed human enough and smart enough to marry. I'd have taken him over most of the boys I knew at school.

6

So Tuck's three-plus years of puppyhood and adolescence had passed, filled with love and fun and a few moments of terror. The longer terror, the terror for Tuck, didn't come until 1956, when I was thirteen and living through that dreadful week when Tuck tore the back screen door and Mother and I knew he had eye trouble.

Going to work or anywhere else, my father always beeped the car horn once when he departed, and twice when he arrived home. It was a little family ritual, so the sinful could stop sinning, he said.

My father came home from Chicago early Friday evening of that dreadful week, beeped twice, and as usual we all went to greet him as he pulled luggage out of the car. Tuck beat us out and jumped up on him.

"You didn't melt, after all," my mother said, kissing him.

The weather reports from Chicago said it had been over a hundred degrees for the whole week he'd been gone, along with high humidity. He should have melted.

He hugged and kissed me and patted Luke on his crewcut. Stan was now sixteen and dating already. That's where he was. Out with a fifteen-year-old brunette.

Luke said, "Didn't even know you were gone, Pop."

Mother said, "Yeah, sure. In a pig's eye."

"You win that game?" Father asked Luke.

"Got two homers." Luke picked up the luggage.

"Hey, wow," said my father, impressed.

What I wanted to talk about was Friar Tuck, not baseball, but Mother always said to give Dad a little while to get his feet on the ground and unwind. This was a crisis, however.

We all started back toward the house, my father with one arm close around my mother, and at the rear steps he stopped and motioned with his right foot at the hole in the screen. "What the devil happened here? Someone kick a hole in this?"

My mother said, "I'll tell you later."

I pleaded, "Tell him now, Mother."

Looking over her shoulder at me, she shook her head. It was a *not yet* shake.

My father went on up to their room to change clothes and begin "unwinding." Fifteen minutes later, having showered, he was back in the kitchen, barefooted and in shorts, his hand wrapped around an icy drink.

He sat down at the kitchen table where Luke was already sitting, his chin resting on the backs of his hands.

I couldn't sit. I was too nervous.

My mother was at the sink, peeling carrots.

My father began to talk about what had happened in Chicago, how hot and humid it was there, who he met and what he did.

I usually liked to hear it all. This time, I didn't want to hear anything and couldn't wait. Finally I blurted, "Daddy, I've got to talk to you."

He said, with annoyance, "Helen, you'll have plenty of time to talk this whole weekend. I'm not going away for another month. You shouldn't interrupt."

My mother turned from the sink. "Tony, we think there's something terribly wrong with Tuck."

My father glanced at Tuck, sprawled out on the linoleum, almost in the middle of the floor, lost in sleep. "With that hound?" he said. "He looks sensational. He jumped all over me tonight. Why, he almost knocked me down."

Mother said, "I know."

"You've got to be kidding," my father said, frowning widely as if we were sounding false alarms. "He could chew on a tiger. Barbara, that dog can run the 100 in 5.2. There's nothing wrong with him."

"There is, too," I said, hoping I wouldn't break down and bawl.

Luke's chin was still on his hands. He gave his

opinion, which wasn't asked for. "Helen, as usual, most of what is wrong is up in your head."

I didn't bother to answer him but gave him a dirty look.

My mother again took a ladderback chair and placed it near the back door. Then she told me to go outside and call Tuck.

It was a repeat performance of Monday, and predictably Tuck jumped up and rammed into the chair again, knocking it aside. He stood there, bewildered, knowing that he'd hit something.

My father was now visibly startled. His mouth sagged. "When did all this happen? I was only gone a week."

"Helen and I think it's been going on for a long time. None of us noticed it."

"You mean he's been bumping into things."

"I'm sure he has," I said.

"It's probably worse with each week," my mother said. "That hole in the door? Happened the day after you left. He went after some cats."

My father was now kneeling down by Tuck, looking at his eyes for a clue. That again.

I said, "You know the doves? They perch up in the trees, and Tuck always barks at them."

My father nodded.

"Daddy, they don't fly away anymore. They just perch up there and look down at him. Or they walk around as if he isn't there. The doves know something is wrong. He can't hurt them now. They know he's harmless."

I rushed over to my father, trying to hold back the

flow of tears. But I was on the watery, choking edge of them almost every time I looked at Tuck now. God and everyone else just couldn't let him go blind.

Mother said, "We've made an appointment with Dr. Tobin for tomorrow."

The night was still thick and warm, and after dinner my parents went out to the patio in back. It was directly beneath my room, and I could hear them talking. I wanted to hear them. I leaned out.

My mother said, "It's incredible. He still leaves every single morning and is gone for his usual hour or so. Crosses streets. Visits the park if he wants. Goes to the store to see Mr. Ishihara. He does exactly what he pleases."

"Including this last week?"

"Including yesterday. He must be able to see some things. Make out images."

My father estimated, "He's going mainly on instinct, I bet."

"It's so dangerous," Mother said.

Yes, it was very dangerous. I knew more about his walks and where he went than they did. I'd seen him cross the boulevard, running swiftly to avoid cars, sometimes dodging between them.

I got down on my bedroom floor beside Tuck to say, "You've always taken care of me, and I'll always take care of you." That was a promise. "And if you can't see, then I'll be your eyes." That was also a promise.

His head was flat against the floor. He was awake,

and his eyes were focused across the room. Or they were looking in that direction.

If only he could talk.

I hated to think about tomorrow. Dr. Tobin was always very kind and gentle with Tuck, but I was afraid he'd tell us some things we didn't want to hear.

I fell asleep on the rug beside Tuck and was awakened a while later by my mother, though I didn't remember it in the morning.

7

Dr. Douglas Tobin was a graduate of the University of California, at Davis, which had one of the finest veterinary schools anywhere. A very tall blond man with a high forehead, big hands, and bony wrists, he always wore a knee-length green medical smock. Even though they weren't human, he knew all his patients by name and seemed to be quite concerned about the health of each one. He'd taken care of Friar Tuck since the first week we'd had him.

Aside from his annual shots, Tuck hadn't needed very much medical attention. He won most of his fights and seldom needed patching up. I do remember that somehow Tuck got a foxtail barb down in one ear his second summer and Dr. Tobin had to put him to sleep to take it out with instruments.

Our appointment was for ten-thirty, and I gingerly led Tuck into one of the clinic's small examination rooms. In the center was a steel-topped table, about waist-high, and in one corner was a cabinet with instruments and medicines in it. A small steel sink was over there, too.

In a moment, Dr. Tobin entered the room and said hello to us, as well as to Tuck, who was always jittery when he came to the clinic. He never failed to wet down the corner of the building before we entered, a nervous reaction.

Dr. Tobin reached down and rubbed Tuck's head, saying to my mother at the same time, "You told me you thought there was some trouble with his eyes, but please tell me exactly what's been happening."

My mother said, "Tell him, Helen."

They'd never retreated from Tuck being *my* dog, my responsibility.

I told the doctor everything that had happened, even about the doves.

He listened intently and then said, "Okay, let's see what's going on here."

He lifted Tuck to the steel table, putting his forearms just behind the front legs and in front of the back legs, lifting him easily, though Tuck was quite heavy.

I had no idea that veterinarians doing eye examinations used the same instruments that are used on humans, but Dr. Tobin peered into Tuck's eyes with an ophthalmoscope, the instrument that looks like a flashlight, with a cone on the end and a tiny light inside.

Standing across the table from my parents, I tried not to show how frightened I was. Earlier that morning, I'd prayed for the first time in a long time. Now, my mouth was dry, my palms wet. I hoped it wouldn't take long.

Tuck behaved very well and only tossed his head around two or three times, pulling away from the instrument. He didn't like it very much when the doctor lifted his eyelids.

Finally, Dr. Tobin rested the ophthalmoscope and thoughtfully scanned my parents, something sad already written on his long face. Then he reluctantly looked over at me. "He has disintegration of both retinas, the part of the eye that receives images."

I didn't know what all that meant. My father did. He stated simply, "He's going blind."

We already knew it, I think, but my knees felt weak, nonetheless. I felt a crushing in my chest.

Dr. Tobin was nodding. I'll never forget his blond head going up and down. It seemed to be in slow motion.

I heard my mother ask distantly, "Can't you do something?" Her voice sounded to me as though it came through an echo chamber. I was in shock.

Dr. Tobin answered, "I'm afraid not," and that echoed too.

"An operation, maybe? By a specialist?" my father said.

I circled around the doctor to stand directly in front of Tuck. He had flattened out on the table, and his head was between his paws. He was like a small child, having no say in what would happen to him.

I finally spoke. "Soon, he won't see at all, will he?"

All three of them looked at me simultaneously. It was almost as if they'd forgotten I was even there.

My father kept on talking. "We're willing to spend the money."

"Yes, we are," my mother said.

Dr. Tobin ignored them completely and said to me, "I want to read you something, Helen. I'll be back in a moment." He left the examination room.

I felt oddly separated from all of them, as if I were somewhere else but still listening to the talk. I began stroking Tuck's head and said, "It isn't his fault," just in case they ever wanted to blame him.

"No, Helen," my mother said. "People, or animals, don't go around causing deafness or blindness. It's nobody's fault."

Maid Marian and Gold Mack shouldn't be blamed either, I thought.

The door swung open again, and Dr. Tobin entered with a thick green book, placing it down on the steel table near Tuck. Leafing through it, he found the page he wanted and said, "Here it is, retinal atrophy."

He began to read, matter-of-factly, "In all instances, the symptoms follow a remarkable pattern of regularity. At first, the animals are shy and exhibit defective vision at night or in dimly lighted places . . ."

I kept rubbing Tuck's head. He hadn't been shy, I didn't think.

". . . the animals bump into objects and move with caution. As loss of vision progresses . . ."

Tuck had bumped into objects.

I tried to listen carefully and to understand the terms.

Dr. Tobin said some other things and then, finally, ". . . there is, to date, no known treatment that will slow the progress of retinal atrophy in canines or effect a cure."

That was really all there was to understand. Wasn't it? Tuck would soon be totally blind!

Dr. Tobin closed the thick green book and reached across to put his strong hand on mine. "I'm sorry, Helen, but it isn't fair to Tuck unless you know exactly what this is all about. I didn't want you to hold out hope."

I said, "I wanted to know." To help Tuck in some way, I had to know.

"How much vision is still left?" my father asked.

The doctor blew out a breath. This was hard for him too. After all, he'd treated Tuck for almost four years.

"With animals, it's almost impossible to tell. Perhaps just faint images. He may be totally blind within six weeks. Then again, three months, six months. I can't say."

"What do we do?" my mother asked.

Dr. Tobin swung his head toward her. "Keep him in the yard. Reassure him you're around. Talk to him a lot. Let him know you love him. Touch him often. He'll need that, your voice and a hand."

I finally broke down. The tears I'd fought so hard against poured out.

Back in the station wagon, mopping my face, I felt destroyed. Tuck was behind me, standing in the luggage space, seemingly happy, his tail wagging, ready to go home. He had no idea what was happening to him, or why. Though he had to be aware that things were shadowy now, or worse, he was reacting as if his eyes were as good as mine. The wide smile was still on his happy face. If ever I would know what heartbreak was, I knew it then.

Sniffling away, I heard my mother say, "I'm going back to pay Dr. Tobin."

My father had already started the car. "We always pay him later."

My mother measured her words, chipping them out. "Tony, we'll pay him *now*. Okay?"

"Oh," said my father, awakening to some other meaning. He turned off the engine and got out too.

I wondered what kind of game they were playing.

Suddenly I knew they were going back into the clinic to talk about Tuck, without me.

Jumping out, I followed them, catching them at the door. I said, "No, you won't."

My mother turned back, her face somber. "I'm sorry, Helen. Yes, come on in with us. But you might not like what you hear."

Not tearful anymore, I insisted, "He can't be put to sleep." That was what I was afraid they were going to talk about.

Sounding as low as I was, my father said, "That's the last thing we'll ever do."

We went inside.

8

We found Dr. Tobin in the pen area of his clinic. Animal patients, large and small, were in their hospital "rooms." We could hear barks, meows, and chirps. Pens lined each side of the concrete alley, which smelled of disinfectant.

If Dr. Tobin was surprised that we'd come back, he didn't show it.

My father suddenly seemed upset. "What the devil do we do now?" His voice was cutting.

"To be very honest, not much," said Dr. Tobin.

My mother was also angry. "That's no answer," she stormed.

Dr. Tobin looked helplessly at her and then at me. "All right, I'll agree that's no answer. I'll give you one. I can put him away, right here. An injection this morning. Now."

I shouted, "No!"

I'd run away with Tuck before I let them do that.

Dr. Tobin went on talking, quietly and calmly. "Or you can give him to the university at Davis. They're working very hard on retinal atrophy."

Mother gasped. "Experiment with Tuck? Operate on him? Make him a medical guinea pig, then kill him?"

"If that's how you want to say it," the doctor answered, with a long, tolerant sigh.

I remember that I wanted to lash out at all three of them until my father, now calm again, said, "We can't even consider that. We love Tuck too much. He's part of our family. He saved Helen's life."

The doctor started to walk, and we fell in beside him. He stopped in front of a cat cage and took out a patient. The cat's head was entirely bandaged. Only its eyes and nose were visible.

"I'm not forgetting that," said Dr. Tobin. "But Tuck might make a lasting contribution to veterinary medicine. He might contribute to a cure for all dogs. We don't get that many chances to work on retinal atrophy cases."

"I'm sorry," said my father, with finality.

The doctor started to walk again, carrying the cat cradled over one shoulder, its eyes peeping out of the gauze. He was stroking its back.

"Absolutely not," my mother agreed.

I had to speak then. "Dr. Tobin, I'd take him away somewhere before I'd let anyone do that."

He looked down at me. "Helen, you may be condemning him to a rope for as long as he lives. I'm not sure that's fair. Think about it."

I didn't know what was fair now. I didn't care.

Dr. Tobin walked into a large room. There was an operating table in there, with straps on it for the animals and a huge light above it. I saw oxygen tanks and those bottles that drip fluid into people or, in this case, animals. I felt uncomfortable in there.

After placing the cat on the table, the doctor began unwinding the head bandage. "Something else you should know. Tuck can turn vicious. He'll live in a world of darkness, and the kind hand that suddenly, unexpectedly touches him can be mangled. He won't expect the touch. Your loving, lifesaving Tuck may bite you. Severely."

The three of us stood silent.

Dr. Tobin continued, "The worst bite I've ever had came from a loving but very blind black Labrador."

"You're trying to discourage us," my father said.

Dr. Tobin smiled. "I'm not succeeding, am I? Okay, on the rope he goes. And you better be prepared to live with it and try to understand it. One dog in a hundred can adjust—can operate solely by smell and sound, in a restricted way. Maybe Tuck can; maybe he can't."

"How long before we'll know?" my mother asked. "Helen starts school next month, and so do I. Teaching, again."

Dr. Tobin replied, "I haven't the faintest idea, Mrs. Ogden. Honestly. You'll just have to observe him."

"But we can't pen him up or put him on a rope now," my father said. "Tuck has always run free, all year around. He's only in the house when he wants to be."

The doctor shrugged. "Then you better prepare yourselves for the worst."

"A car hitting him?" my mother asked.

"The chances will increase each week he runs loose."

By this time, Dr. Tobin had fully unwound the bandage, and we could see that the cat's head was completely bald. There was an ugly red scar crowning the gray skin of the skull.

Dr. Tobin said, "Here's a car victim for you."

9

Whenever my mother worked on the flower beds, she usually wore blue corduroys and a faded T-shirt that said, "Arm Bears. Don't Bear Arms." She was cultivating her marigolds and petunias at this moment, digging into the rich brown earth with a metal claw. We hadn't been home from Dr. Tobin's too long.

Mother always worked around her flowers when she was upset, claiming the fragrance and bright colors of the blossoms and the feel of the damp earth helped chase personal clouds away. I watched her awhile and then went inside, Tuck padding along behind me.

My father was in the den at the desk, his fingers gliding over the old adding machine. He paid all the bills in our house, being good at math.

The furniture in that room was white wicker covered in a flower print, but my favorite was a large white rocking chair from Hickory, North Carolina, where my grandmother lived. I sat down on it, and Tuck flopped down on the large oval braided rug on which the chair rested.

I had a lot on my mind, and rocking always helped.

I asked my father, "What's it like to be blind?"

I couldn't see him but could hear his voice.

"Terrible, I guess."

I was curious about something else. "Is it better to be born blind or go blind later?"

He didn't speak right away. Finally he said, "Helen, I can't answer your question. I just don't—"

Then the phone rang in the kitchen, and Stan yelled, "Dad, telephone."

Saved by the bell, he left the room, while I kept rocking, thinking that if it were me, I'd much rather go blind later on. Then I would have seen everything, known exactly how things looked and what the colors were. Of course, color didn't matter to Tuck at all. I'd learned long ago that all dogs are color-blind.

Stan edged into the room. He said, "Hey, Sis, Mom told me about Tuck and what happened at the vet's this morning. I'm sorry. I really am. I've done a lot of kidding about you and that dog, but I love him too."

I looked up at my towering oldest brother and nodded.

Then he knelt down to pet Tuck, rubbing under his front leg-pits where he always liked to be rubbed.

"So, if you want to go off somewhere, I'll sit with him."

That bothered me, although I'm not sure why. I looked straight at Stan and said, "He doesn't need 'sitting with,' like a baby."

"Well, I made the offer," he said and departed.

I relented and yelled after him, "Thanks."

Then Luke came into the room with his soccer ball. He dropped it and sat on it, balancing in the doorway while he talked.

He said, "Helen, I'll help you walk him if you want me to."

Suddenly these two household males, who gave me a loving but bad time most of the time, were being nice to me. It was all because of Tuck.

I made a grunting noise and kept on rocking.

Luke asked, "Are his eyes going to turn funny? White? Or will they be gooshie gray?"

"No one knows," I said.

Luke said, "That blind man who runs the newsstand at the post office has gooshie gray eyes."

That was awful. "Luke, do you need to talk about it?"

He said, "I gotta go," and picked up his soccer ball.

I rocked some more and decided to go up to my room. I wanted to try something. Tuck got up and followed.

I wanted to know exactly how Tuck would feel when he had to go everywhere and see nothing. I realized that he would have an advantage over me because he could smell things I couldn't. Who else but a dog can smell a dove? I also assumed that his hearing was much better than mine. He could hear sirens long before I heard them.

Inside my room, I closed my eyes very tight and began to walk around, bumping first into my bed and then into my chest of drawers. I refused to open my eyes, no matter the bumps. Suddenly I tripped over Tuck and hit the floor, and then my eyes opened wide.

My mother was standing in the doorway with folded arms and raised eyebrows, monitoring me. She asked, "Helen, just what in the world were you doing?"

"Trying to see how Tuck would feel."

"He might feel a lot better if you didn't step on him."

I said, "I had my hands out to feel my way around." Then I added stupidly, "Tuck doesn't have hands."

"Most dogs don't," my mother said. "Stan just came out in the yard to tell me he thought you were cracking up. I hope you're not."

I was not about to crack up and said so. Or maybe I was already cracked up.

Monday morning, I did something that I seldom did in summer—I got up early. My father awakened me after his alarm clock in the master bedroom went off, and I dressed hurriedly. It was six-thirty.

Tuck was already at the back door when I came down, and my mother let him out, as usual. But this time, he had a follower—me!

I waited a moment and then went on his trail, hoping that he wouldn't be aware I was behind him. There wasn't any wind blowing, so whatever odor I had wasn't wafting up toward him.

Wanting to see how he navigated by himself every

day, I made up my mind not to call him or let him know I was around unless it was absolutely necessary.

Tuck moved surefootedly along the sidewalk and grass strip as if he had 20/20 vision, going at a slow trot up Cheltenham, stopping frequently to sniff and leg lift. There were royal palm trees with thick trunks in the strip, and he seemed to know exactly where they were. Maybe he had radar in his head?

He went for half a block without hitting anything, but the DeFords, at 816, hadn't taken in their empty garbage cans from the trash pickup, and I watched as Tuck plowed into one, head on. It rolled and banged in the dawn.

He stopped and seemed to be staring at it, then sniffed it and went around. More than anything else, he seemed to be embarrassed at knocking it over.

Denham Boulevard was the next cross street over, and I was tempted to call him as he reached the curb there. Early morning traffic was already zooming by on Denham. He paused and seemed to be listening to it as the cars whined past us.

I held my breath. Would he do it?

At last, he turned away from the curb and went up Denham, as if he weren't sure enough of himself to cross at that hour. Maybe later. I breathed again.

I continued to follow him on up Denham to Wickenham, the street that paralleled ours. He made a right turn there, and I was running by that time to keep up with him.

Without warning, he dropped off the curb and began to angle across to the other side of Wickenham.

Suddenly I saw a car coming our way, fast.

I yelled at him, and he stopped, turning his head sharply to look back in my direction.

My mother had been right, as had Dr. Tobin.

Our Tuck was living dangerously.

At dinner that night, my mother said to my father, "Now, if you want to go to the lake for Labor Day, let's make the plans. Don't wait until September first." My Uncle Ray had a cabin at Lake Angeles, and we usually went up there for hot dogs and potato salad, swimming and trout fishing.

My father nodded but didn't answer.

I'd been thinking about something all day, ever since seeing Tuck pause at the curb on Denham and then watching that car speed toward him on Wickenham. Maybe I had a solution to Tuck's trouble?

I said to all of them, "You know I have to start school in three weeks. Nobody will be home, and Tuck needs someone to take care of him."

My mother looked at me uncertainly. "A dog-sitter?"

My father commented, "That's not necessary, Helen. We can't afford that kind of thing. I think he's learning to adjust."

I'd told my mother about the car on Wickenham in the morning. She muttered, "Learning to adjust to jeopardy."

"I don't mean a dog-sitter," I said. "I've been thinking all day about what he needs. He needs one of those dogs that help the blind."

No one said a single, solitary thing. Silently they all just turned, together, and looked at me as if I were bedbug crazy. Four enemy heads aimed in my direction.

10

Because I didn't think it would do much good to talk to my family anymore about a helper dog for Tuck, I stopped by Ledbetter's on Tuesday to visit Mr. Ishihara. Always an optimist, he immediately said it was a brilliant idea.

"What can you lose?" he asked.

Nothing at all, I thought.

So, afraid of getting into an argument if I made the call at home, to be overheard and reported on by Luke, I stopped by the public phone booth opposite the doughnut shop at the busy corner of Rosemont and Denham, spending forty cents of my own precious money.

"California Companion Dogs for the Blind, Inc.," was listed in the white pages.

The woman who answered the phone there switched me to the office of the administrator, a Mrs.

Mary Chaffey, and in a moment I was talking to Mrs. Chaffey's secretary, who sounded very businesslike. My goal was to help Tuck, through any means I could.

Without hedging around, I said, "I'd like to make an appointment to talk about a companion dog."

"Is there someone in your family who is blind?"

"Yes," I said flatly, knowing full well she thought I was referring to "someone" with two legs.

"You sound awfully young," said the secretary.

"I'm not that young," I replied. "I'm thirteen."

The secretary asked, "Is your mother or father there? You sound as though you're calling from a phone booth." The traffic was indeed whizzing by. Tuck was sitting patiently just outside the half-open door.

"I am," I readily confessed. "My parents are home. But they need an appointment. They're too embarrassed to call you."

Right away, I noticed a marked change in her attitude. I guess she thought they were poor, old, and blind and too proud to call, so their little girl was doing the calling.

She said, softening up, "Oh, my, they shouldn't be too embarrassed to call us. That's what we're here for. What's your last name?"

"Ogden."

"Tell them five o'clock Thursday. The appointment will be with Mrs. Chaffey. But please phone me back if they can't make it. Do you need transportation? We'll provide that too."

I said we didn't.

Deciding it would be unwise to announce the arrangements at the dinner table, with my brothers around, I told my mother just as soon as I reached home.

"They gave you an appointment?" she marveled, sounding as if she didn't quite believe it.

"It's for you and Dad."

"And you told them about Tuck?"

For a very good reason, I didn't answer that question directly. I just nodded and said, "They understand about dogs."

"I guess they do," my mother agreed. "I'll talk to your father. I'm really surprised."

That night at dinner, my father laughed about it. He seemed pleased, too. He said, directly to Stan, "See? You want things done, you have to do them yourself."

Then to me, he said, "What time's the appointment?"

"Five o'clock Thursday."

Under the table, I crossed my fingers in the special way, two over one on each hand.

Stan said, shaking his head, "I would've bet anything they'd tell her to drop dead." Luke wasn't at home, or he surely would have said something similar.

Mother chided Stan. "It's a well-known charitable organization, and I'm sure they don't go around telling anyone to drop dead."

Stan shrugged.

For the next two days, I thought mostly about that school for companion dogs out in San Carlos. I wondered what the school charged for the dogs. What kind they'd be. How old. If I had to give up my entire allowance until I went to college, that would be perfectly okay. But I thought that once they took a look at Tuck, they'd be glad to give me a dog free of charge. Occasionally, as Luke said, I built things up in my mind. Everything was rosy when I did that.

On Thursday, my father came home about a quarter to four, since it took an hour to reach San Carlos, a little town out in the country in another county, with a lot of dairy farms around it.

Waiting in the driveway for his two beeps, I rehearsed myself. Then up he rolled, and I said, "I have something to tell you," the moment he unwriggled from the small car.

His eyes narrowed. He could always guess when I was about to make a confession. He listened and then sighed. "Now, why did you have to do it that way?"

"Because I thought the school might not even talk to me unless I told a white lie."

He shook his head with disappointment and said, "It wasn't so white," then went on inside.

In the station wagon, waiting for them, I said to Tuck confidently, "We're about to solve your problem."

In a few minutes we were on our way. I was in the back seat, of course, with Tuck, staying silent, crossing my fingers and doing some praying. I'd done a lot of double finger crossing in my lifetime but not so much praying.

After a while, my mother turned to me to say, "I'm still surprised they gave you an appointment."

Observing me in the rearview mirror, my father said tartly, "I'm not."

"I don't understand," Mother said.

"She told them you and I were 'too embarrassed' to make the call. She also told them that 'someone' in the family was blind. She didn't say *who*. I also get the impression that the school thinks we might be indigent, since they offered us transportation."

I shut my ears.

My mother looked first at my father, then at me. "When did you learn about all this, Tony?"

"She confessed ten minutes ago."

My mother swung her full attention back to my father. "Why didn't you tell me? Now, I am embarrassed. They'll throw us out."

I pushed farther back into the seat.

Father said, "We're committed. We might as well try now."

Mother glanced at him once again and then back at me, her eyes bleak. "Helen!"

I silently set my jaw, determined to let nothing bother me. The most important thing on earth was Tuck. Not them. Not me. Just Tuck.

Finally, several miles out of San Carlos, where dairy farms were scattered around low rolling hills, we saw a big wooden sign with a full-sized black Labrador painted on it. "California Companion Dogs for the Blind, Inc." was lettered above the inky Lab, marking an open gateway. We drove through it.

The moment the car engine was turned off, we could faintly hear many dogs barking but we couldn't see them. In a pretty setting of lawn and shade trees and pathways, there seemed to be a half-dozen low gray-shingled buildings, across from a parking lot.

We sat for a moment, just looking around.

"If it weren't for all the dogs barking, you'd think it was any good private school," my father said.

"It certainly isn't your average private school," my mother said, nodding toward a green van that had just pulled up to the entrance.

Six or seven blind people, with their companion dogs, stepped from the van and began walking up a pathway toward one of the bungalows. We could hear them laughing and talking, the dogs moving along with them.

A troubled look creasing his face, my father turned to me. "Helen, this place is for humans with catastrophic problems."

I clamped my jaws. Nothing was going to change my mind.

My mother said, "Are you really sure you want to go in there?"

I took a long time to answer, then said, "Tuck has a catastrophic problem too."

"Okay," sighed my father, reaching for the door handle.

I advised Tuck, "We won't be too long," and got out too.

My mother said bitingly, "That's an understatement."

Just inside the door to the administration building was a fat black Labrador with a graying chin and whiskers. His tail was wagging as we went inside, stopping a moment to pet him.

The receptionist said, "Henry is our greeter dog. He's ten years old and retired."

I thought to myself, that's the very kind of dog we need. Being ten, he'd had a lot of experience. He'd be perfect to guide Tuck around. But since he was the "greeter dog," I doubted that he was for sale.

My father asked for Mrs. Chaffey, and we were directed down the wide hallway. There were several other older dogs lolling around, sleeping in the hallway or padding down it. In fact, retired companion dogs seemed to be plentiful, and I was now almost certain we'd drive away with one.

In a moment, we were ushered into Mrs. Chaffey's office. Dressed in a white blouse, riding breeches, and boots, she was a tall, slender woman with silver-gray hair and silver bracelets on her right wrist. Smiling, she asked us to sit down, explaining that she was going riding in a little while. "We keep a few horses here. It's the right country for it."

I looked around her office. On one wall were large photos of four different types of dogs. On another wall was a huge blackboard labeled, "Area Status." Names of dogs and people were on it, along with dates. From outside, we could hear all the yelping.

Mrs. Chaffey glanced toward the window. "It's feeding time, and they're always noisy for that. But they're awfully good at night. We have a big population here. More than three hundred at all times, of all ages. German shepherds, Labrador retrievers, black and golden Labradors. Those types make the best companion dogs, we've found."

My father said, hesitatingly, "The blind people we saw when we came in, are they . . ."

"Students," she said. "We take them to nearby towns or the city six days a week, with the dogs. It's very routine. They're here for twenty-eight days of intensive training with the companions we've selected for them. Then they graduate." She paused.

"Now, how can we help you, Mr. Ogden?"

My father was visibly embarrassed. He said, "Ah, well. Well, ah. Do you ever sell any of these dogs?"

"Oh, my, no. Never. We breed them here. Send them to farm families for more than a year for human contact, then bring them back and train them, and finally lend them to blind people."

"There's no charge?" my mother asked.

"None at all," replied Mrs. Chaffey. "We're entirely supported by public donations and endowments."

Then she looked at my father, trying to get to the point, and asked, "A member of your family is involved?"

I blurted it out. "Yes, my dog, Tuck. He's blind."

She blinked, and her mouth opened helplessly. In what seemed like forever before she did speak, she looked over at my mother and father. They were squirming.

Then she said, "I—you see—I hardly expected . . ."

She stopped, cleared her throat, and started over again, looking straight at me. "I'm so sorry to hear that."

I said, "Isn't there one real, real old one, like Henry, that you could sell us for Tuck? We'll take good care of him."

Mrs. Chaffey said, "I know you'd take good care of him." She nodded toward the board. "See the dogs up there, with the masters and mistresses by each name, and the date we graduated those teams?"

I looked up at the board.

"When a dog retires at about the age of eight and is replaced by a younger dog, the retired dog often stays with the blind person's family or goes back to the farm where it lived for a while. Or, in a few cases, retires here like Henry and the others you saw in the hall. They become the pets of staff members."

"I'd hoped there'd be just one . . ."

Mrs. Chaffey said, "Helen, our dogs are so very special. We select only the best, and it costs more than six thousand dollars to train each human-dog team. Our contributors would be outraged if we sold a companion dog. You must understand."

Though I swallowed and nodded, I had to lower my head to hide the deep disappointment. I'd been so certain they'd sell us a dog for Tuck.

Mrs. Chaffey went on. "And, you know, I've never heard of a companion-type dog being teamed with a blind dog. I'm not sure it would work."

I lifted my head. "Would you like to see Tuck?"

Mrs. Chaffey rose from behind her desk. "I'm fond of all dogs."

We went out to the car, and I opened the back door. Tuck jumped out, that yellow flag of a tail thrashing around.

I said to Mrs. Chaffey, "This is Friar Tuck Golden Boy. He's three and a half years old."

Tuck smiled in our direction.

Mrs. Chaffey put her hand to her mouth, as if her breath had been whisked away, murmuring, "He's so beautiful."

Though Tuck was smiling at her, his eyes were vacant and useless, beginning to turn that "gooshie gray" that Luke had talked about. No wonder she was upset.

"He's a very good dog, too," I added.

With anguish, Mrs. Chaffey said to my mother and father, "Can't anything be done surgically to help him?"

Father answered, "We've been told, by a very good vet, that there's no hope for that. He advised us to either put Tuck away or give him to the animal medicine school at Davis."

Mrs. Chaffey shook her head and said, "I wish so much that I could help you." We could see how distraught she was.

She said to me, "Thank you for letting me meet Tuck. I must go."

She hurried back into the administration building, and none of us spoke very much on the way home.

My grand idea had fallen apart.

11

About a week after the unproductive visit to the companion-dog school at San Carlos, just a few days before my school started, Mother let Tuck out for his usual morning stroll at about six-thirty.

Tuck started off as he did on any other morning, loping down the driveway, but less than ten seconds had passed when Mother heard the sickening screech of car brakes and a muffled yelp. Instantly she guessed what had happened and called out to my father, who was upstairs, shaving. Then she ran outside, still in her blue robe and scuffs.

A car was stopped in the middle of Cheltenham, about fifty yards from our house, and in front of it was poor Tuck, on his side on the pavement, a still gold mound. Maybe dead. The driver of the car was kneeling down.

My mother ran to Tuck, and then my father, having

pulled on his robe, joined her. There was blood on Tuck's head, and he was quivering, breathing in short gasps, blank eyes still wide with fright. Fortunately the car had struck him a glancing blow as it skidded to a stop, only the bumper hitting him.

The driver, a student on his way to college classes at Los Angeles State, was very upset, saying, "The dog suddenly ran out in front of the car, as if he hadn't seen me."

"He couldn't see you," my father said.

Stan had heard my mother cry out and had awakened me. I came downstairs in my nightgown just as my father and the young driver were carrying Tuck to the station wagon. I saw them through the kitchen window. They had Tuck in a first-aid carry, with their hands locked on each other's wrists.

My mother was already on the phone to Dr. Tobin.

As I rounded the corner of the house, my father took one look at my chalky face and said, "Helen, don't panic! He's alive. He's hurt, but he's alive." Closing the back door to the station wagon, he added, "Maybe you shouldn't look at him. I have to get some cotton. I'll be right back."

I'd never been very brave about anyone getting hurt, or seeing blood. I'd always turned away, feeling faint. But this time I made myself do it, opening the wagon door instantly. I almost wished I hadn't.

Tuck was on some beach towels that my mother had thrown down, and I saw that the gash on his head went from behind his left eye all the way to the back of his right ear. Blood was oozing from it, and the yellow hair was already matted. Tuck was shaking all over, as if freezing.

He needed me, I knew.

Climbing in beside him, I pulled one of the towels around him, then began stroking his side and belly, telling him again and again that everything would be okay. I tried not to look at his bashed head.

Having put some clothes on, my father came back with the surgical cotton and began pressing it against the wound. He asked how I was doing. He knew about the willies I always got when I saw blood. I said I was doing fine, but I wasn't at all. I thought I might faint. Yet I surprised myself that morning.

Stan soon relieved me, stroking Tuck while I dressed, and then we rode to the clinic, like attendants in the back of an ambulance, my mother doing the driving.

Tuck was in surgery by seven-thirty, wheeled in on a cart.

Mother and I sat anxiously in the waiting room for more than an hour, but it seemed like weeks. It wouldn't have been much worse if Stan or Luke had been stretched out on the table in there. Unable to shake the fear of Dr. Tobin coming out to say Tuck had to be put to sleep, I fidgeted and kept going to the water cooler.

Mother said, "Calm down."

I couldn't.

Finally the doctor did come out, saying, "He's bruised mostly, and I had to do some stitchwork. He now has a crown of sutures."

"He'll live?" I asked.

Dr. Tobin laughed heartily, which was reassuring. "Sure, he'll live. You can pick him up tomorrow. I put him under, of course. He'll be groggy for the rest of the day. I want to watch him for a while."

Crisis over, my mother glanced at me. "Tuck is just plain lucky," she said.

"Maybe you'll take my advice now and pen him up," said Dr. Tobin. "He won't survive many of these."

Next day, we picked up the patient, and aside from where his head had been shaven and the wound stitched up, he didn't look much the worse for having lost to a car bumper. He was limping, though, because of bruises, and Dr. Tobin said to let him set his own rate of recovery. He was still very sore and tender.

12

Tuck did take it easy for a few days, during which time I started back to school. He went no farther than the backyard for his morning stroll, or he stayed safely in the kitchen or den. Or up in my room. He'd learned his lesson, we all thought. No more tours over to Denham or Wickenham; no more going to the park by himself, or visiting Mr. Ishihara, crossing the streets.

Tuck, however, always had other ideas.

On Sunday morning he apparently felt well enough to jump the fence and take his usual prowl of the neighborhood, even with the black curlicue stitch ends still crowning his stubborn head. One minute he was safely out in the yard, sniffing around, and the next he was gone. He departed while my mother was fixing waffle batter. She just happened to see that flag of yellow tail fly over the fence.

Next thing I knew, my father was shaking me

awake, none too kindly, and telling me to go find my dumb dog.

I found him, all right, ambling without concern along Wickenham, as if cars had never been invented, as if he didn't have an ugly scar on his half-bald head. I scolded him, but he stood there looking at me with those useless eyes, his tail wagging.

What was I to do? Hit him for something he'd been doing all his life? I couldn't. But that short Sunday journey surely cost Tuck his freedom.

My father was waiting with a long rope when we came home, and he said, "Helen, I've had all the scares this week that I'm going to have. And, believe me, we're not going to make a practice of visiting Dr. Tobin every few days. Tuck will stay in this yard whether he likes it or not."

Tuck had never been on a rope. I said, "It'll kill his spirit."

"Better to kill his spirit than to have him kill himself in the streets. Right?"

Yes, that was right.

He'd already tied the rope to a clasp, and that was snapped to Tuck's collar. The other end of the rope was tied to a water pipe that ran around the base of the house.

I said, "Can't we make the fence higher, Daddy?"

He shot back, "No," and stomped off.

He seemed to be angry with both of us, but my mother said, a few minutes later, that he was just frustrated. He was truly worried about Tuck's safety.

I stayed out a little longer and watched Tuck as he encountered the new enemy. He couldn't see what this was for, but he certainly felt it. Walking to the end of the rope, he was suddenly stopped, with a jar. He turned, as if trying to figure out what was holding him, then barked at it.

I went to him and tried to explain. But how do you tell a dog that something is being done for his own good, especially a dog that looks at you out of dead eyes?

I was now beginning to understand what Dr. Tobin had been talking about.

After breakfast, I watched Tuck for a while from the kitchen window. He was like the tigers at the zoo, pacing and pacing. He'd go to the full length of the rope, only to be jerked back. Then he'd pull against the enemy, his strong front legs braced against the ground.

Unable to stand it any longer, I finally went out and took him off the rope and up to my room.

Seeing us troop up the stairs, my mother advised, "He's got to learn, Helen."

"He doesn't have to do it all in one day, though, does he?"

"He'll be alone here tomorrow," she reminded.

In the morning, after Tuck was put back on the rope, one by one we all went off, my father first.

My school, Montclair Elementary, was less than a mile away, and I usually departed last, walking it each day. I made certain that Tuck's water bowl was full because Septembers in Southern California are nearly always hot. Then I knelt by him to hug him and tell him to be good; I'd be back soon.

Throughout much of the day, I worried about him and then ran straight home—to be greeted in the backyard by Friar Tuck, *off his rope.* Only a few frayed feet remained on his collar. He'd chewed through it.

Though I did talk to him about it, there wasn't much use in scolding him, shaking a piece of rope at him, or yelling that he was a bad dog.

Instead, I got a snack of oatmeal cookies, which he dearly loved, and off we went to the park.

On the way home, I stopped by Ledbetter's, and Mr. Ishihara volunteered that Tuck had paid him a visit in midmorning, dragging that short length of rope. "I didn't take it off, so you'd know he chewed through it."

"We put him on it yesterday. We had to do something."

Mr. Ishihara knew all about Tuck's collision with the car. "Maybe you'll have to keep him inside every day until you come home."

"He wouldn't like that."

"Maybe he must learn to like it. Be positive with him." Mr. Ishihara was beginning to sound like my mother.

I didn't have to tell my father that night that Tuck had mangled the rope. It was all too evident. I also admitted that he'd gone over to Rosemont and Ledbetter's.

"Well, he'll now lose another privilege," my father said, with stony intent.

Tuck would now have to spend most of the day locked up in the house, to which he'd never been confined. And that meant he should have a long walk before I went off to school. So I set the clock-radio alarm for a quarter to six.

Never one to jump eagerly out of bed and greet the sunrise with a smile, I remember I struggled up and dressed in a daze the next morning. It was still dark outside, which made no difference to Tuck, of course. He sat on my bedside rug, staring anxiously in whatever direction I went, sensing he was about to have a treat.

My room was next to my parents' bedroom, and Father appeared in the doorway in his polka-dot pajamas, blowsy and frowning and blinking. "Helen, what are you doing?" he asked.

"I'm taking Tuck for a walk."

"At this hour?"

"Somebody has to do it," I said heroically.

He went away, and I heard him grumbling to himself, "It's still dark out there. She shouldn't be walking the street."

Then I heard my mother soothing him. "Tony, come on back to bed. You've got another half hour."

"Thanks," he said.

I went downstairs and out. The morning paper hadn't even been delivered.

Again that night, my father complained about my walking Tuck in the darkness and now would not let me go out until after daylight, cutting the time we had for his exercise.

Then, on Thursday, I came home to complete disaster.

Walking up the driveway, I always yelled, like my

father and his beeps, letting Tuck know I was home, so he could stop sinning. Then he'd run to the back door from wherever he was inside, and wait, tail waving.

That day his tail wagged vigorously all right but I knew something was wrong the moment the door swung open. He'd sinned. Splinters of wood were all over the floor. He'd tried to chew his way out. Chunks of wood had been torn from the back of the door. Teeth marks were also on the door handle where he'd tried to open it. Splinters were on the sill and floor by the kitchen window.

Tuck had been a one-dog wrecking party while I was in school.

I talked to him, telling him that he'd done something very bad, but I still couldn't bring myself to hit him, though I wanted to. Waiting to be walked, tongue hanging out, he sat there looking at me with those sightless eyes. I had to pity him.

Tears of helplessness leaked out of my own eyes as I swept up the debris. A lot of damage had been done, and I dreaded having my mother walk in; even more, my father. I decided not to take Tuck out and to await our fate.

An hour later, Mother, a bag of groceries in her arms, surveyed all the destruction and said, "Oh, Lordy." She sat down weakly at the kitchen table and said to Tuck, "What'll we do with you?"

I thought she might be furious with him, but she seemed to feel more the way I did—just helpless.

My father was angry for a moment or two but also ended up shaking his head in despair.

I offered to pay for all the damage, but he just groaned.

However, on Saturday, Father installed thirty feet of heavy steel chain, attaching it to the foundation of the house. I saw him testing it, heaving back on it, and it was plain that a two-ton Percheron would have trouble with it.

Tuck was stopped.

I passed my mother in the downstairs hallway that gloomy morning and said, "I hate that chain already."

She answered calmly, "We're not in love with it either. It's necessary, Helen."

The rope had been bad enough, but now to have Tuck shackled to steel was almost more than I could bear, or watch, despite all the problems.

Day after day, Tuck fought back. He went to the chain's full length and pulled against it, as if he were pulling a sled. Or he'd turn the other way, rearing on his hind legs the way a wild stallion fights a rope in a corral. He would try to pull the choke collar from his neck, over his head and ears. The fur around his neck was being worn off.

Failing to break the chain or get loose from it, he paced in a long, tight oval, wearing the grass away. Though Tuck himself never made a sound, we could hear the clanking of the chain from inside the house and knew that Tuck was waging his lonely battle. Within a month, not a blade of grass was growing where he paced.

It was terrible to watch and hear. When I was home, I walked him for hours, just to keep him off the hated chain. I kept up walking him every morning before school; then after school, I'd run straight home and have him off the chain within a few minutes, sometimes not even going to the bathroom. My mind wasn't on school or books, and my grades, which had always been good, began to slip.

Other inner things were happening to me, I guess. Even my brothers were worried, I suppose. Stan said, "Hey, Sis, you don't whistle anymore. I miss it." They'd always been the first ones to hassle me about the tweeting.

One evening just before Thanksgiving, when my brothers weren't around, my parents sat down to talk to me about a lot of things, mainly Tuck and myself. They talked about school and my grades; then they talked about my health. Finally my father said, "Helen, maybe we should seriously think about what Dr. Tobin said, about giving Tuck to the university at Davis. He's more than any of us can handle now . . ."

Stricken with grief, I ran from the room. My best defense now was to run.

Then, just before Christmas, I was in the den. There was a half-written letter on the desk from my mother to my grandmother, back in North Carolina. I read some of it:

> *. . . It has been three months since we put Tuck on the chain, and he's finally given up. He no longer has the will to resist. He fought the chain valiantly, even wearing all the grass away. But, at last, we have subdued him, and none of us is proud.*

*Helen's mind hasn't been on school or books,
and she's doing very badly. She is "Nurse
Helen" or "Mother Helen" or counsel for the
defendant. At times, I think she blames us
for what is happening with Tuck. We cannot
go along this way for very much longer . . .*

I didn't read any more.

It was raining hard that chill afternoon but I decided to take Tuck for a walk anyway. After I got a
half block from 911 West Cheltenham, I repeated to
Tuck that I'd never let *anyone* take him to Davis or
any other place like that. Nor would I ever let anyone
put him to sleep. The two of us would be long gone
before that happened. Just where, I didn't know.

13

Two nights after New Year's, I happened to overhear a conversation that was taking place in the den. Passing by the door, I heard my parents talking, and unfortunately I listened for a few seconds before going on upstairs. Dangerously, I didn't hear the beginning of the conversation or the end.

What I heard was: "Tony, I'm just not willing to start another year of this. Her health is too important." That was my mother's firm voice. She'd made up her mind about something.

"All right, I agree. I'll call Dr. Tobin in the morning." That was my father talking, of course.

In my frame of mind, that was quite enough to hear. I pulled away from the door and hurried up the stairs, already convinced that Tuck would either be put to sleep or be given to the doctors at Davis for experimentation.

Until that long and mostly sleepless night, I'd never thought about running away from home for any reason. Knowing I was loved, I only had to look around my room to see I was properly cared for. The thoughts of being somewhere else just never occurred to me.

But the months of worry about the yellow-haired dog with the pinkish nose, now safe and sound asleep beside me, suddenly went off with a silent bang. Looking back, I'd been preparing myself for this crisis ever since the Saturday morning in Dr. Tobin's clinic when Tuck was pronounced to be on the brink of blindness.

Likely, the idea had been building steadily even though I don't think I was aware of it. Now it was time to go, for Tuck's sake.

I thought about calling my grandmother in North Carolina for help but knew she'd be back on the phone in two minutes asking my mother, "What in the world is that child thinking about?"

Mr. Ishihara? He'd do the same thing, I knew. He'd never let me stay in his apartment or help me leave town. He'd quickly call 911 West Cheltenham.

Though Tuck was welcome in the homes of most of my friends, there wasn't a one, including Steffie Pyle, who would take us in because of this trouble.

Tossing around in bed, I'd never thought so hard in all my life. By ten o'clock I'd sorted some things out and, considering my age then, I believe the sorting was very correct and even wise. Transportation for a thirteen-year-old girl and a blind dog was not going to be easy, no matter the destination.

Buses do let blind people and guide dogs aboard; but I didn't think the drivers would accept the reverse. For a while, I had in mind just showing up unannounced with Tuck at my grandmother's in Hickory, North Carolina. By that time, say after a week of travel, my parents would know just how desperate we were, and they might change their minds.

I ruled out airlines right away. That kind of money was not available, and the airlines would put Tuck in a box down in the cold cargo space.

Hitchhiking along a freeway was certain to bring a highway patrol car sooner or later, and a call to my parents. Besides, I was not too keen on sticking my thumb up, anyway, and it would take a real dog-lover to stop and load us in.

There was only one choice left, a terrible one—walking.

Only where to?

I guess it was almost midnight when I finally decided what to do and where to go—temporarily, at least, until I could make long-range plans. My Uncle Ray's cabin at Lake Angeles was closed for the winter, but I knew I could break into it. He had a lot of canned goods stored there, so we'd have plenty to eat; there was always a big stack of firewood on his porch, so we'd have heat. Though snow was on the ground up there from December to March, it was never too deep.

Lake Angeles was fifty-five miles away, but I figured we could walk it in two days.

Just after I made the decision to hide out at Uncle Ray's for a while, I went to sleep.

In the morning I tried to act as if it were any other day—taking Tuck for an early walk, having breakfast, dressing for school. As the family went off, my father first and then my brothers, I said good-bye as if I'd be there for dinner, as usual.

Then the station wagon, bearing my mother, backed away and I ran upstairs to pack a TWA airline bag, taking underwear, socks, an extra shirt and pair of jeans. I planned to dress warmly for the walk up the mountains. I'd been on that road many times in the summer but only once or twice in the winter.

I talked to Tuck occasionally while pulling everything together, though I was talking more to myself, I suppose, trying to think of what I should take. I had a dollar and forty cents in my top bureau drawer and stuffed that into my pocket. There was always money in the kitchen.

Down there, in the utility drawer, where housekeeping bills were tossed and car keys dropped, I found eleven dollars more and added that to my treasury. There'd now be plenty for food until we reached Uncle Ray's. Then I packed a lunch.

Not once did I think about doing anything wrong. My goal was to take Tuck away from danger, and nothing else mattered.

My final act that morning, just before nine o'clock, was to write a note to them all, and that was the hardest part. I told them I was doing this to protect Tuck and hoped they'd understand. I signed it, "Love, Helen and Tuck," then gathered my parka and the airline bag, into which I'd placed the lunch, and out we went.

I had vague plans to be on the other side of Glendale and Pasadena, where the Crest Highway starts up into the mountains, by nighttime. I was a little worried about where we'd spend the night, but with Tuck along I knew I'd be safe. We could sleep almost anywhere.

I took one look back at 911 West Cheltenham, wavered a moment, and pressed on.

That January day was unusually sunny and warm. The parka which I was carrying and the airline bag in my right hand became heavy before we'd gone a mile.

By noon, when the temperature must have been seventy degrees, I was almost out of it. My feet hurt, and we stopped on the other side of Griffith Park, over in Glendale, at a hamburger place with outdoor seating. I ordered a burger for Tuck and ate the lunch I'd packed, just to lighten the load.

For quite a while I'd been hoping that someone would stop us and ask, "Where you going?" but no one had paid the slightest attention. We'd passed a patrol car parked on Los Feliz, and the cops had only looked at us, saying nothing.

We went on slowly and, for me, painfully.

I can still see myself that late afternoon as we reached the outskirts of Glendale, nearing the beginning of the Crest Highway. With Tuck moving along at my knees, each step hurt. My arms ached from carrying the bag and the parka; my legs ached, and I'd worn a blister on my left heel. I hurt all over.

I sat down for a while, wondering if I should try to hitchhike or pay someone to take me up the mountains, which were already turning blue in the distance.

The sun would set within a half hour. The longer I sat, the more I knew I could never make it to Uncle Ray's, that night or the next.

Finally, surrendering, I got up and dialed 911 West Cheltenham and said, "It's me," when my mother answered.

What came out of the phone next was a mixture of relief and anger. They'd called the police, for one thing. Furthermore, I was informed that they'd been talking about Dr. Tobin consulting with experts at Davis to see if there was any last possibility of surgery for Tuck. They weren't talking about putting him away.

My father picked me up at the filling station, where I'd made the call, shortly before six. He said, "Maybe this will teach you not to eavesdrop."

In addition to being sore and tired, I felt very foolish.

14

The rains started again in mid-January when winter storms from the Pacific, driven by high wind, came ashore to wet down Los Angeles off and on for about ten days. I clearly remember those days because of sloshing along the sidewalks in my red boots with Friar Tuck. It was just too muddy to visit Montclair Park.

I also remember coming back from a damp sidewalk tour one of those afternoons—the exact date was January 16, 1957—to find my mother waiting for me in the kitchen.

She said, withholding news, "Go hop in the car."

"Where are we going?"

"You'll see."

So Tuck and I went out to the station wagon, and in a moment we were gliding over the slick streets.

"Remember Mrs. Chaffey?" asked my mother.

Of course I did. She was the woman at the San Carlos school.

"She called just after I came home."

Mother took her eyes off the road a second. "There's a dog that they may retire."

My heart beat a little faster. "That's where we're going?" Under my breath, I said, "Oh, God, thank you."

My mother nodded.

"Will they give us a dog?"

"I don't know. She didn't say. She just said we should come out there if we were interested."

"You said we were?"

My mother laughed. "What do you think?"

"I wonder what kind of dog it is."

"Does it make any difference? They only train the four types."

It made no difference. I would have taken a purple poodle guide dog, and I don't really like poodles, especially little ones.

Mother went on. "Now, don't get your hopes up high. Last time you moped for days."

How could I keep from getting my hopes up? They'd gone up out of sight already.

Mother kept on talking, driving through the pelting showers. "Even if they do lend us a dog, it may not work. Remember Mrs. Chaffey said she didn't think it had ever been done before."

I finally refused to believe that it wouldn't work and said so. How did anyone know?

I sat there as the bright green winter countryside, washed in rain, whirled by, already positive that Tuck

could be led everywhere by the companion dog. Such
was my faith.

In just over an hour, we eased through the entrance
to the school and went directly to Mrs. Chaffey's
office, saying hello to old Henry on the way.

She said, "I suppose I should be surprised that
you'd drive this far in bad weather, but I knew you'd
come. I've thought of Tuck so many times—I couldn't
get him out of my mind."

She stood and crossed over to the big status board
and put her finger on one particular line. "Lawrence
Stafford," she said. "He was in his early seventies and
died of a heart attack this morning."

By Mr. Stafford's name was another name, *Lady
Daisy*.

Mrs. Chaffey went on. "He lived alone in an apartment in Irwindale, which isn't too far away, and the
paramedics took his dog to the animal shelter. One of
our trainers picked her up around noontime."

Lady Daisy! I thought. Heaven had sent her to the
rescue.

Mrs. Chaffey went back to her desk and sat down.
"I remembered Tuck . . ."

Balanced on the edge of the chair, I held my breath.
My mouth had gone completely dry. Daisy!

". . . and wondered if you still had the problem. If
you do, we might think about lending Daisy, who was
Mr. Stafford's companion dog."

Words rushed like spilled beans. "Tuck's problem is
bigger than ever," I said. "He's on a chain. On rainy
days, he's locked in the garage. He eats the doors and
windows. He stays in trouble and gets me in trouble."

Mrs. Chaffey laughed. "I'm sure you don't want that. So, would you like to see Daisy?"

I was standing upright before Mrs. Chaffey could even finish the sentence.

We followed her out. The dogs were noisy, since it was once again near feeding time.

The kennel buildings were long and low, with high chain-link pens extending out from each side, so the dogs could have outside air and sunlight when they wanted it. Each pen had a little open doorway to the inside of the kennel building for bad-weather sleeping and living.

As we went along, Mrs. Chaffey said, "We have kennels for the mothers and their puppies. Also places for the puppies during their testing period. We test them for reactions to strange sounds and obstacles, as well as general intelligence."

"Some are rejected?" my mother asked.

Mrs. Chaffey nodded. "Then we have kennels for the dogs in training after they've been out with farm families for a year and a half. They're here for about six months, including the time they train with their blind masters or mistresses. They have to learn to work in harness and master all the commands."

"Has Daisy done all that?" I asked.

"She was born here, tested here, and then spent eighteen months with the McIver family in the Imperial Valley. Then she was six months back here again and was graduated, along with Mr. Stafford, in 1953."

We stopped by a small office building to add a trainer to the party. Introduced as Harry Peterson, he had a leather dog leash wrapped twice around his hips, like a belt. It was easier than carrying it everywhere, he said.

Momentarily, we turned into one of the kennel buildings, full of happy, barking dogs, and about eight pens down, we stopped. So did my heart and whole body.

There was Lady Daisy, sitting on her haunches, looking at us through the triangles of pen wire. She was a brown and black German shepherd and had soft, kind eyes. A little chubby, she looked like a very motherly dog.

She's so right for Tuck, I immediately thought. Saint Lady Daisy!

While Mother and I stood in the aisle between the long rows of pens, the trainer and Mrs. Chaffey went inside. Mrs. Chaffey squatted down by Daisy, asking the companion dog, "How would you like to retire at the age of six?"

Daisy was very dignified, standing quietly, wagging her tail in response, looking in my direction.

Then Mrs. Chaffey said to the trainer, "She's really too old to start retraining with a new master, isn't she?"

Peterson answered, "Borderline, at best."

Then Mrs. Chaffey said to Daisy, "I think I know of a super home for you and a super job."

Harry Peterson said, "I trained her well."

Mrs. Chaffey smiled up at him quizzically. "Well enough to guide a blind dog?"

"Oops," said the trainer.

Mrs. Chaffey arose. "Daisy, I'd like you to meet some people."

Then she brought Lady Daisy out, and I sank beside her on the concrete floor, whispering to her, "Wait until you see Tuck."

She turned her lovely head to look at me, full face, and there was an ancient calmness in her brown eyes, as if she knew many things.

I heard Mrs. Chaffey saying to my mother, "Even under normal circumstances, we'd retire her in another two years. The dogs begin to lose their sharpness about the age of eight. But Daisy has a lot of life ahead, I think."

I looked up. "Can we take her home today?"

"I'm afraid not," Mrs. Chaffey said. "She has to have a good physical. We also have to make inquiries about your family. This is all highly unusual, and it can't be done overnight. Next week sometime, I'd guess."

There would never be a longer wait in my life.

15

The arrival of Lady Daisy at 911 West Cheltenham the following Monday was loudly, angrily announced by none other than Friar Tuck Golden Boy himself. He knew that a canine intruder was on his front porch, and he set up a din in the backyard, straining at the very end of his chain.

Daisy followed Mrs. Chaffey through the door as if she were two-footed and totally human, and then she sat down politely by Mrs. Chaffey's feet and looked around as though inspecting her new house.

My mother said, "That's the most sedate, serene dog I've ever seen in my entire life."

Soon, that most sedate, serene dog met the entire family, excepting Friar Tuck, who was, or had been, the full opposite of Daisy on many occasions. On this late afternoon, he was unserenely making enough noise for a pack of barking wolfhounds.

I went out to shush him.

When I returned to the living room, my mother was saying, "I'm worried that Tuck might resent her. Plain jealousy. Listen to him now."

"That's a real worry," Mrs. Chaffey admitted.

I asked, "You mean Tuck might not let her stay here?"

"Yes, that's possible," Mrs. Chaffey said. "He might even hurt her. He's a very powerful dog."

"I wouldn't let that happen," I promised.

"You can't be around them twenty-four hours a day. And if Tuck really wanted to hurt her, I doubt you could stop it."

"I'll teach them to be friends," I said.

"That's a good start," she replied. "But there's no instruction for what you're about to do. Another thing, you and you alone should be the trainer. It's always best that way. One person doing it."

My father said, "Suppose Tuck and Daisy just don't get along."

"Well, the answer to that is simple," Mrs. Chaffey replied. "We'll place Daisy in another home or take her back to the school. We never abandon these dogs, under any circumstances."

My father said, "Okay, let's see how Mr. Tuck reacts."

We all went out to the backyard, and Tuck, fur standing in a ridge on his back, growled the moment the door swung open. Unable to see, he'd smelled Daisy, and even though she was female, she was intruding into his space nonetheless.

Mrs. Chaffey quickly said to me, "Talk to him, reassure him."

I commenced talking fast, telling him Daisy wanted to be his friend, but the low, throaty growling went on as Tuck circled her, tense and suspicious. Daisy stood absolutely still as he inspected her, sniffing and sizing her up.

The growling worried me, and I said sharply, "Behave, Tuck!" I'd seen some of his wild fights in the park, and they'd begun that way, growling and circling.

"How do I do it?" I asked.

Mrs. Chaffey looked at me. "You're the trainer, Helen. But I'd go slowly. Very slowly. You can't force friendship—humans or dogs."

She departed for San Carlos a few minutes later, extracting a promise from my parents to call her at the least sign of trouble.

I stayed out in the backyard a while longer, just watching the activity. Tuck soon seemed to lose interest in Daisy and clanked over to his favorite sleeping spot by the house. She then lowered herself to the walk by the back steps and closed her eyes too.

Deciding to take Mrs. Chaffey's advice to go slowly, I did nothing with Tuck and Daisy that night except feed them in separate bowls, well apart from each other.

By bedtime, when Mother came into my room, Tuck was in his usual place on the rug beside me, and Daisy had taken up a neutral position in the middle of the floor.

Sitting down on the edge of my bed, Mother said, "Well, tomorrow you start an adventure. A big one."

I said that so far Lady Daisy had been very careful. "Not drinking out of Tuck's bowl. Not taking Tuck's place here by the bed."

"She's obviously an extremely intelligent dog. Now, Helen, don't ask too much of her—nor of Tuck; nor of yourself, for that matter."

I said I wouldn't, though, of course, I really wasn't listening to that kind of instruction.

"We'll be rooting for you."

"And for Tuck?"

Mother smiled. "Daisy, too."

Most everyone I know who owns a dog talks to him or her occasionally, or even frequently, but aside from the few basic commands, I don't think the exact words count for too much. The tone of voice means much more, along with the movement of one's hands. The latter did not apply to Tuck now. Looking back, I see that I talked a lot to him over the next weeks. Pleaded might be a better word. Whether he understood or not, he began to display almost every bad trait there is. Selfishness, jealousy, anger, pettiness. I could go on for a page. He was an awful dog for quite a while.

As soon as I arrived home the next afternoon, I brought Daisy out of the house and unsnapped Tuck from his yard chain. He chose to ignore her, as if she didn't exist.

I then led Daisy up to his side, positioning her so that his big ears were about opposite her ample rump.

I then said to him, "Tuck, put your head against her," and simultaneously pushed his skull her way.

A tremendous roar of anger and defiance rumbled from deep within him. His jaw was open, and his fangs were bared. Those sightless eyes were aimed in my direction, and there was a glare in them of a strange kind. There was no love in them.

I jumped back. He hadn't bared his teeth at me since he was a pup. This was another Tuck I was seeing and hearing—maybe a frightening one. I remembered Dr. Tobin saying that the worst bite he'd ever had was from a blind Labrador.

Go slowly, Helen, Mrs. Chaffey had said, and I told Tuck, "Okay, we'll just take a walk today."

I put leashes on both of them, and off we went. Again trying to ignore Daisy, Tuck growled only when she bumped him. But it was evident that he didn't at all like sharing his walk with Lady Daisy.

On the way home, I stopped at Ledbetter's to pick up a box of small dog biscuits, putting them on our charge account. They were to be rewards for accomplishments.

Mr. Ishihara wanted to know how the training was progressing, how "they" were doing. I said it hadn't started as yet, but "they" weren't likely to be any problem. It was "he," bullheaded F. T. Golden Boy, who might mess up the whole idea.

He proved it a few minutes later when he arrived home. Making threatening noises in his throat, he refused to let Daisy enter the house. He stood in the doorway, hair up along the ridge of his neck, his whitish-gray eyes staring at her. Was I going to be afraid of my own dog?

Daisy had been trained to resist attack by remaining completely passive, and she stood quietly with her front paws on the steps, looking away from him as if to say, I will not allow you to upset me.

As was known around our house, I seldom had yelled at Tuck for anything, but this time I did. Finally, like a lion in the jungle, he retreated unhappily deep into the kitchen, and we went peacefully inside. He was beneath the kitchen table and pouting, following us by sound.

Day after frustrating day for almost two weeks, I attempted to train Tuck to put his head against Daisy's rump, the first step in teaching him to be guided by her. Day after day I failed. Aside from an occasional sniff, he refused to have anything to do with her. Force certainly did not work. Though he didn't bite her, he growled mightily and exposed those big ferocious teeth. She remained cool and passive and didn't even flinch.

Day after day, I also saw someone or another watching my failures through the kitchen window. Now, nothing can make you angrier than being spied upon when you are losing. And each night at the dinner table, I was asked how I was doing, and my answer was a tight-lipped "Fine," though it was evident I wasn't doing fine at all.

My mother would see me coming in from the backyard after a frustrating session and say, "Keep trying, and don't get angry with him."

How could I help but get angry?

There was a vacant lot about six blocks away, over on Wickenham, and I finally took the dogs there, just to avoid the snooping "told-you-so" eyes in the kitchen window.

I remember I was holding Daisy's collar in my left hand and Tuck's in my right, positioning myself on Daisy's right flank, to walk them around the lot, which had some gravel scattered here and there. I started them off, and Tuck immediately lunged forward, pulling me off balance. I took a header into the rocks.

When I reached home, Luke asked, "What happened to you?"

My face was scratched up. I lied about it, saying I'd walked into a tree branch.

"Hah," said Luke.

On Saturday, I was in the backyard again. I snapped a leash on Daisy and then took another leash and attached one end to Daisy, the other end to Tuck. Maybe if she towed him along, he'd get the idea of what it was all about. But when I attempted to lead her away, Tuck promptly backed up and sat down, donkey-style.

I went over to him and whacked him hard on the back, hurting my hand more than I'd hurt him. Yet I hadn't hit Tuck for years, for anything, and here I was, feeling terrible remorse. Kneeling down, I said, "I'm sorry, Tuck. I didn't mean to do that."

My father heard me. He came boiling down the steps and said, "Don't apologize! He's misbehaving even if he is blind. Don't feel sorry for him—belt him."

That was easier to say than to do.

Another week went by, and the following Saturday the family went to the beach minus Stan, who was boxing groceries at the supermart as usual for that day.

We always went to the beach several times during the winter for a picnic. With only surfers in the cold water and very few other people around, the beach was almost as much fun in the winter as in the summer. We brought wood for a fire. The wind off the Pacific that February day was chill, the sky was gray, and the waves were pounding in.

As soon as we arrived, I opened the back of the station wagon, and the dogs leaped out, free to go as fast and as far as they could. They began running and sniffing along the dune line of the deserted beach. Though each went freely on individual explorations, they stayed within a few feet of each other. They were a pretty sight, bounding along, the wind whipping at them.

The four of us—my parents, Luke, and myself—walked several miles south, watching the dogs and the diving sea birds and keeping a lookout for whale spouts. After staying in Mexican waters, the gray whales are on their migration back to the Arctic in February and often swim close to shore, the newborn calves pumping along beside them.

Eventually we returned to where the station wagon was parked and started the fire in a ring. Everyone remembers days from childhood, and this one stands out for me. The wind was twisting the smoke away, and a fine salty spray, almost a mist, was blowing in

from the sea. Our faces were red, and hair was a tangle.

After the leisurely picnic meal, my father said, with no warning, "Helen, you saw how well Tuck and Daisy got along today. We think it's time to let the dogs just be friends. No more training."

I'm sure that was one of the reasons he wanted to take us to the beach—to tell me exactly that.

"Give up?" I asked, in alarm. They couldn't ask me to do that. I wouldn't do it, anyway.

"Yes, give up," Mother said. "You've tried so hard for almost two months, and nothing is working. I talked to Mrs. Chaffey yesterday. She agreed with your father and myself. Just let them be companions now. No more training."

"But I—"

My father interrupted firmly. "Now listen to us, Helen. Your schoolwork and your mental health are more important. I'm sorry but that's true."

"Tuck will stay on the chain," I protested.

He nodded. "Probably. Yes. Forever, maybe."

"I have to—" I began, feeling panic.

He interrupted again. "For everybody's sake, you *have to stop*. You tried very hard."

Mother added, "And we're so proud of you."

Those words, or words like them, have been said to daughters and sons since the cave days, I suspect, but they don't take you off the hook of failure.

That night I whispered into Daisy's ear, "We won't stop."

In fact, I already had something else in mind. By

now, however, I wouldn't discuss with anyone anything I was going to try. They were all defeatists, except Mr. Ishihara. But the previous week I'd seen an old circus picture on TV, and in it some elephants were walking along in their traditional parade way, trunk to tail entwined.

I went into Luke's room to ask casually, "Don't you have a book on elephants?"

Without even looking at me, he motioned to his shelf. "It's over there."

I pulled it out and went to my own room, where the two dogs were sleeping peacefully, and got into bed with *The Book of Elephants*.

16

To keep prying, snoopy eyes out of my dog business, I went to the very end of the park, over where Wickenham takes the long curve toward Wilshire. A high hedge of white-blooming oleander separates the park from the street at that point.

No one in my family would ever see me there, I thought, and I could continue to train Tuck in complete secrecy. How wrong I was.

As soon as I arrived, I took Tuck's seven-foot leash and attached it to Daisy's collar, then attempted to make Tuck grasp the looped end in his teeth. He flatly refused to even open his mouth.

Once I'd seen Dr. Tobin open Tuck's wide jaws quite easily by applying pressure at the very back, at the hinges. I put my fingers back there, and Tuck's mouth opened like a trap. Sticking the leash end in, I pushed his jaws together and held them a few seconds. Of course, he dropped the leash as soon as I took my hands away.

Trying to be patient with him, I said, "All right, we'll start all over again."

We did the same routine a half dozen times daily for two or three days, and it turned out the same each time. Tuck stood there and opened his mouth, accepted the leash, and then dropped it right out. By Friday, I believe he thought it was a game we were playing, and much fun.

Put the leash in!

Drop the leash out!

Friday was also the day that Luke accidentally discovered my secret training place. Something was wrong with his bike, and he decided to walk it through the park instead of going along the Wickenham curve. He came through a hole in the oleander hedge like a hawk searching for a rabbit, and there I was, holding Tuck's jaws closed on the leash.

Pushing his bike up to me, my brother, having caught himself a criminal, said, "You're not supposed to be training those dogs."

I replied, "Luke, I'm only doing what I have to do, and don't you dare tell anyone." Now that I was thirteen, I didn't let him push me around so much.

"Aw, who cares?" he said and went on his way.

That night, just before dinner, when I was alone in the kitchen with my mother, she said, offhandedly, "I hear you're still training Tuck and Daisy."

Curse Luke anyway, I thought. I knew things about him that I hadn't told anyone. I knew things that could get him into so much trouble.

"Are you?" she asked.

What could I say? "Yep."

Eyeing me as if trying to make up her mind, she said, "I should be angry."

I just stood there, waiting for whatever was going to come—the firing squad or A for effort. It should have been the latter.

She laughed softly. "Any luck?"

I shook my head. "But I can't give up."

"Never be so definite about anything," she said. "Okay, I won't tell your father, and I've told Luke to quit spying on you. But I'm giving you a firm deadline, Helen. Two weeks more, and then no more."

That was fair enough, and then I told her about my elephant idea.

On a firm deadline now, with no time to waste, midmorning of the next day I went over to see wise Mr. Ishihara at Ledbetter's. He was in the back storage room, which always had a dozen good pungent smells wafting around it. Boxes of fruit, burlap sacks of potatoes and carrots, small mesh bags of onions, and coffee beans were in there; canned goods were stacked to the ceiling. Sawdust was on the floor.

Bent over, using a small crowbar to open a wooden crate of lettuce from the Salinas Valley, Mr. Ishihara listened to Tuck's latest unwillingness to cooperate.

"He drops the leash out. He thinks it's a game," I said.

"Try rubbing some food on it."

I hadn't considered doing that.

Mr. Ishihara straightened up suddenly. "Don't, on

second thought. It's a bad idea, very messy, and he might chew on the leash."

Knowing Tuck, I figured that was a distinct possibility.

Mr. Ishihara, pursing his expressive lips, wrinkling his smooth walnut forehead, examined me for a moment longer and then said, "I've told you about my cat, Ichiban, haven't I?"

"Yes, you have."

"He likes to sleep on my dirty shirts. I think he likes to smell me."

My own dainty Rachel had never done that, to my knowledge.

Picking up the opened lettuce crate by its ends, Mr. Ishihara continued, "Ichiban gives me an idea for Tuck. Suppose you put something of your own on the leash. Tuck can't see what it is, but he'll definitely smell it."

I followed him out of the storage room. "Like what?"

"Like your shirttail, but don't wash it," he said, over his shoulder. "Leave it dirty and just tear it off." Moving quickly to the sidewalk stands, he dropped the crate by his lettuce bin and laughed loudly. "The way to Tuck's stubborn brain may be through his nose."

That made good sense. How much I appreciated Mr. Ishihara.

The next day I cut off the end of the shirt I'd worn to school on Friday and went to Montclair Park, ready to tell anyone that training a blind dog was a very long, difficult, and frustrating thing to do. If I hadn't owed Tuck so much, I probably would have given up on him.

I tied the rag around the hand loop of the long leash, snapped the leash on Daisy's collar, and then dropped the wadded end to the ground right under Friar Tuck's pinkish nose.

"Pick it up," I ordered.

Tuck stood there, as usual, motionless as a hairy sphinx. Be positive, I thought.

Reaching down to guide his head, none too gently, I repeated, "Pick it up, Tuck."

He sniffed the rag several times, then opened his jaws, and, lo and behold, grasped the leash end firmly.

For a moment, I was so surprised I didn't react, but then I finally woke up and said sharply, "Forward, Daisy."

She started off, with Tuck in tow, the leash end between his shining rows of teeth.

Daisy was walking along as if she did this every day in the week, probably just the way she'd walked with Mr. Stafford.

After so many weeks of struggle, it had finally happened, like a snap of fingers. Tuck could come off the hated chain at last.

"Stop, Daisy," I yelled joyously, and she halted on the dime, so to speak, with a front paw almost in midair.

Tuck stopped in his tracks too, dropping the leash end and standing over it as if nothing had happened —the dumbo.

Running over, I hugged them both and gave them

their due biscuit rewards. I felt giddy, like telling the whole world, but I said to them, "We'll not tell a soul until we're ready."

I wanted to see Daisy guide Tuck *without a leash*.

Tuck soon began to enjoy the fabulous new trick he'd learned—that of picking up a stinky, wadded rag between his teeth and trekking along behind the well-padded female he'd previously either ignored or snarled at. Time and determination did it, without doubt.

But by twilight I noticed that Tuck had trouble locating the leash end if it was on the ground more than three or four feet away.

I went right back to Mr. Ishihara.

After a moment studying the dogs, he said vaguely, almost to himself, "Tuck can't see, but he can smell and he can hear."

I said, "Sound!"

He nodded. "Sound."

Up on the shelves in the back of the garage were large cartons containing Christmas decorations, and in one of them, I knew, was a long, narrow piece of leather. Attached to it were eight small brass bells, for placing on the front door. Our wreaths were always on either side of the door.

That night I rummaged through the Yule boxes and found the bells. Next day, in the park, I wired one to Daisy's collar. I thought she might object, but she didn't even seem to notice the bright bell tinkle each time she moved.

I still had the shirttail, damp with Tuck's saliva, tied

to the leash, and I ordered Tuck to pick it up. He nosed down, and then I said to Daisy, "Forward."

With Tuck moving along about three feet behind Daisy, leash firmly in his mouth, the little bell rang as though it were on the harness of a sleigh horse. A jingle-bell sound. I walked behind them as we went the length of the park.

Each day that week I shortened the leash until Tuck's head was directly opposite Daisy's rump. He now seemed content to trot along with her, his left ear rubbing conveniently against her flank, listening to her bell as if it were a symphony.

17

About that time, the "Colonel Bogey" march was being played on all the Los Angeles radio stations because of the 1957 Academy Awards. The music is from the movie *The Bridge on the River Kwai*, starring William Holden and Alec Guinness, about prisoners of war in a Japanese camp and the blowing up of a bridge they'd built over the River Kwai.

I'd seen it.

The troops whistled as they strutted along, their arms swinging the way British soldiers always do it when they march to a big brass band. *Whee-who, whow, who, whow, whee-whee, who* . . .

I loved it, especially the whistling *whee-who* part.

Anyway, having set my clock-radio, I woke up to all the tweeting and brass band from the *Kwai* movie the next morning, and I got out of bed quicker than on most weekends.

Immediately I said to the two dogs, who were sitting patiently side by side on my rug, gazing up at me as if I were queen of Cheltenham Castle, "Do you understand that today is the most important day of your whole lives? Of mine too?"

I was talking about Tuck getting off the chain forever, of course.

Naturally, neither one of them knew precisely what I was saying, but their tails wagged just the same, and I have an idea that they knew something sensational was about to happen.

While in my nightgown, I took them out in the yard for a short johnny session and then brought them back inside, having planned, to the hour, what I'd do that morning.

Maybe I'd felt better in my lifetime, but I couldn't remember when, and the day outside matched it all. The California sky was cloudless and desert blue, and the strong sun was already warming everything, drying the dew.

Looking at myself in the bathroom mirror that morning, I remember deciding I wasn't so hideous after all in this thirteenth year on earth. I still wasn't any raving beauty, but I'd improved somewhat, I thought. Even my mouth didn't seem so much like the Grand Canyon anymore, and I think some of my freckles had gone off wherever they go.

I dressed and was having cold cereal when my mother padded down to the kitchen in her robe, heavy-lidded and yawning. There'd been a party the night before. She mumbled a good morning, surprised to see me up and around and in street clothes this early on a Saturday. I was always the sleeper.

I said a cheery good morning to her and then asked casually, "Are you going anywhere today?"

She was foggy. Heating water for coffee, she turned, frowning as if she didn't understand me. She was always one of those people who seem to float out in space until they have their first cup of coffee. After that, they are sharp.

I repeated myself and said, "It's important that you're here at ten-thirty."

"What's happening?"

"You'll see," I said, refusing to say more.

She yawned. "Aw-right."

I awakened Luke and told him to have our parents, along with himself, out on the front lawn at ten-thirty sharp.

"Do you hear me?" I asked.

"Um. Yeah. Yeah." He rolled over but was awake now.

So, in high spirits, I departed 911 West Cheltenham a few minutes later with Tuck and Daisy, bound on a trot for Montclair Park and what I hoped was the finale of two months of hard and dedicated labor.

Wasting no time once I arrived, I knelt down to take off both dogs' leashes. This was it, I vowed. Freedom for Tuck Day!

To him I said, "Okay, no more leash. You're on your own, baby cakes. Put your yellow head up against Daisy when she starts off, and don't you dare do otherwise."

Those sightless eyes were riveted on me, and I think he understood.

I added, "No more fooling around, Tuck. Today's the day."

I had to be positive with him. Pity never worked. Maybe positive would.

Daisy was watching us, and I simply said to her, "You know what to do, big mother." No question about that.

Then I maneuvered Daisy up beside Tuck, so that his head was near hers. Without bothering to cross my fingers, which I'd learned gets you nowhere, I stood back and shouted, "Forward, Daisy."

She began to move, the little bell on her collar rang, and Tuck trotted after her, at last placing his head firmly against her rump.

I let out another yell. I'd won! I'd finally won!

If I'd had angel wings and pearly toes, I would have taken off across the lake. Instead, I just ran after the dogs, a lot of sticky stuff suddenly in my throat. But it was certainly no time to cry.

They were truly a sight to see—Lady Daisy, her head held high, ears up, and Friar Tuck Golden Boy, matching her step for step, guiding on her flank. That's the way we went jingling across the park, and the early morning onlookers applauded.

I practiced with my students for almost an hour and then checked my watch. It was twenty minutes after ten, time to head home.

The "Colonel Bogey" march was still rattling around in my head, and I said to them, "We're going to do this like a parade."

Soon, we went whistling past Ledbetter's, and I thought Mr. Ishihara was going to throw his tomatoes up into the sky in celebration.

At Denham we waited for the stoplight to change and, almost a block ahead, I could see my mother and father out on the lawn by the sidewalk. Luke was there too.

Then we stepped off, and I said to my troops, "Pass in review," and began to whistle the march from *Kwai*.

I was swinging my arms the way Colonel Alec Guinness did in the movie, and suddenly I realized I wasn't walking—I was strutting.

I began to feel that I wasn't just a girl with two dogs walking behind me, but a whole victorious army with flags flying. A full brass band was there marching up Cheltenham, the sun spanking off the tubas and trumpets, the drums booming and rolling. Jets were screaming in from above in salute.

I heard Luke's yell, "She did it!"

Up the street we came, the dogs moving at a steady pace, Daisy heeling behind me. I looked back at Tuck. His head was high too. He was not about to lose his dignity.

I noticed something else. Tuck wasn't just smiling. The dog with the Dudley nose and gooshie gray eyes was grinning.

Soon, Luke began to yell. "Yea, Helen, yea! Yea, Tuck! Yea, Daisy!"

I'd never felt so good. So confident. So beautiful.

Fic
TAY

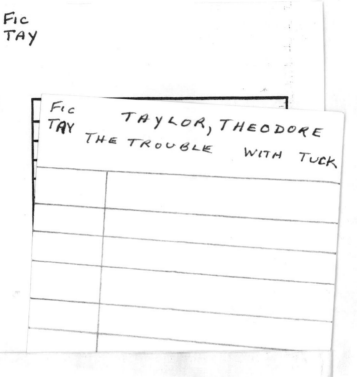

Fic
TAY   TAYLOR, THEODORE
     THE TROUBLE   WITH TUCK